CORPUS DELICTI

David Brunelle Legal Thriller #6

STEPHEN PENNER

ISBN-10: 069242976X
ISBN-13: 978-0692429761

Corpus Delicti

Joy Lorton, Editor.
Cover by Nathan Wampler Book Covers.

THE DAVID BRUNELLE LEGAL THRILLERS

Presumption of Innocence

Tribal Court

By Reason of Insanity

A Prosecutor for the Defense

Substantial Risk

Corpus Delicti

Accomplice Liability

A Lack of Motive

Missing Witness

Diminished Capacity

Devil's Plea Bargain

Homicide in Berlin

Premeditated Intent

Alibi Defense

Defense of Others

Necessity

CORPUS
DELICTI

corpus delicti. *n. (Latin, literally, "body of the crime")*

1. the substantial and fundamental facts (as, in murder, actual death and its occurrence as a result of criminal agency) necessary to prove the commission of a crime;

2. colloquial: the body of a murder victim.

Merriam-Webster Dictionary
11th Edition

CHAPTER 1

The office of King County homicide prosecutor David Brunelle was silent, save the occasional squeak of a highlighter across a police report and the unrelenting din of the thoughts racing through his mind.

He was distracting himself with the bad decisions of others in order to avoid consideration of his own mistakes.

The phone rang.

His eyes flew to the caller I.D.

But it wasn't Kat.

It was Chen. And Brunelle knew it wasn't a social call. Seattle P.D. Detective Larry Chen hadn't been social with him since Brunelle had broken up with Kat Anderson, assistant medical examiner and all around great gal. Ordinarily, Chen probably would have sided with his friend of a dozen years, but it was the way Brunelle had ended the relationship that had angered Chen. By Brunelle not ending it before starting another. And lying about it.

That new relationship was over too. Dying a sad, pathetic death literally days after Brunelle chose it over his one with Kat. So now he found himself alone, not nearly distracted enough, and picking up the phone to talk to someone who used to be his friend but now pretty much hated him.

"Brunelle," he answered the phone with just his surname. He was trying to sound cool and detached, not angry. He wanted Chen to stop being angry, more than anything.

Well, more than almost anything.

"Uh, hey, Dave," Chen started. His voice was the truly cool one. Cool and distant. "I tried calling Fletcher, but he wasn't in. Nicole said you were available."

Brunelle grimaced. *Good ol' Nicole*. One part legal secretary, two parts counselor.

"Nicole was right," Brunelle answered, trying to sound comfortable. "What can I help you with?"

There was a pause. Brunelle wondered if it was indicative of Chen being irritated at the suggestion of needing help, or of Chen reconsidering whether he really wanted help if it came from Dave Brunelle.

"We've got a situation down at the station," Chen finally explained. "It might be a homicide."

"Might?" Brunelle repeated. "You don't know?"

"Well, it's kind of hard to tell," Chen said. "That's why I'm calling."

Brunelle's eyebrows knitted together. Was this some sort of trick to get him to call Kat? "What does the M.E. say?"

"The M.E. isn't involved," Chen answered.

That made no sense. "How is the medical examiner not involved? Any time there's a suspicious death, they take custody of the body."

"That's just it, Dave," Chen finally explained. "There is no body."

CHAPTER 2

Seattle P.D. didn't have just one station, of course. The city was twenty miles north to south, stretched across a collection of hills and peninsulas. Every neighborhood had a precinct, and there were even a couple of police storefronts in the bigger malls. But when Chen had said 'the station,' Brunelle knew exactly what he'd meant: the Public Safety Building downtown on 5th Avenue. It was a 14-story, glass-and-steel skyscraper, home to the Seattle Municipal Court, the Seattle City Council, and, on the first floor, the main offices of the Seattle Police Department, complete with holding cells and interrogation rooms. Brunelle met Chen next to Interrogation Room Number 3, presently occupied by a slightly disheveled and extremely frightened young woman.

"That's our killer?" Brunelle asked incredulously, jabbing his thumb at the frail woman on the other side of the two-way mirror. "She doesn't look very murderous."

"That's 'cause she's not the killer," Chen replied brusquely. "She's a witness."

"A witness to the murder?" Brunelle asked. It was good to have an eyewitness to a murder. Not common, but good.

"Not exactly," Chen answered. Then the smallest smile crept into the corner of his eye. Whatever else might separate them now, there was still the bond for solving crimes and holding offenders accountable. Justice.

The detective nodded toward their witness. "It would take too long to explain. Just watch and listen."

Then Chen stepped out of the observation room and back into the interrogation. Brunelle got as comfortable as he could in the small, chairless room; he crossed his arms and shifted his weight solidly onto one foot.

"Sorry about that, Linda," Chen apologized as he closed the door behind him and sat again at the small table he shared with the young woman. "I had to check in with someone on a different case. Can we just start again from the top?"

Part of the problem with coming into a story halfway through was not quite knowing the cast of characters or previous scenes. It made listening more than just listening—it was like solving a puzzle. That was part of the fun too.

"I—I don't know, Detective Chen," Linda responded, her voice high and her cadence quick. "I think I said too much already. Can I just go? I really think I better go."

But she didn't make any effort to stand up. She was waiting to be released, like a trained dog in a 'sit' command.

Chen raised a calming hand. "You're safe here, Linda. No one's going to charge you with anything…"

Brunelle raised an eyebrow. That was a prosecutorial decision. He didn't appreciate Chen writing checks on his account. On the other hand, despite their recent tension, he still trusted Chen. It just whetted Brunelle's appetite for the puzzle.

"…and no one will know what you said. It's just for me. It's just for Amy."

That raised two questions for Brunelle. Obviously, who was Amy? And less obviously, but perhaps even more importantly, who was she worried was going to find out what she said?

Chen's assurance seemed to be working, but it was a little hard to tell. Linda was clearly under the influence of something. She was having trouble sitting still, her eyes were distant but darting, and when she spoke, she spoke fast.

"If no one's gonna know what I said, why do I have to say it?"

A fair question, Brunelle had to agree.

"No one's going to know you said it," Chen repeated, "but I need to know it. I need to find Amy."

Linda stared at Chen for several seconds, then started shaking her head a bit too vigorously. "You're not gonna find Amy."

Ah. Brunelle finally understood why he was there. And who Amy was. She was the victim. He decided to remember that name. 'Amy.' Too often cases got called by the killer: 'State v. Smith.' 'The Smith case.' But this one was going to be the Amy case.

Still, he wondered who the defendant would be. Judging by Linda's appearance, intoxication, and fearfulness, Brunelle had a guess. Her pimp. And Amy's too. Puzzle solved.

"Kenny's not gonna find out, Linda." Chen leaned forward onto the table. "I'm gonna book you on soliciting, the D.A.'s gonna close it without charges, and you'll be out tomorrow morning. You'll get a night off, and he'll never know why you were really here."

Linda looked down and nodded, slowly this time despite the probable methamphetamine in her system. "I'll pay for that night off," she mumbled.

Brunelle frowned. He knew she was right. All the more

reason to hook up this 'Kenny' for Amy's murder ASAP.

"When was the last time you saw Amy?" Chen asked. Brunelle knew this was for his benefit. Chen had already heard it. That's why he'd called the D.A.

Linda hesitated a moment and kept her face lowered, but she answered. "Three weeks ago. She got into a car with Kenny. He was so mad at her. He was already beating on her before he even put her in the car. Somebody else was driving. I don't know who. But he pushed her in the back seat and climbed in after her, hitting her the whole time."

"Why was Kenny hitting her?" Chen followed up.

"He thought she was holding back on him," Linda answered. She looked up again. "She wasn't, though. She gave him everything. She just couldn't earn that much any more." Linda frowned as she considered speaking ill of the presumably dead. "It's harder for some girls to get dates."

Dates, Brunelle thought ruefully. Like it was two kids at the malt shop or something.

"Did Kenny come back?" Chen continued the questioning.

Linda nodded. "It took a while. I'd done two dates by the time he came back. He was sweaty and his clothes were dirty. One of the girls asked him why and he just punched her in the mouth. I didn't ask shit. I just got into the next car that pulled up."

"Was Amy with him?"

Linda smiled weakly. "No, Detective Chen. That's what I told you. That was the last time I seen her. That was the last time anyone seen her."

Brunelle knew Amy was dead.

He also knew Kenny murdered her.

And he knew it would be next to impossible to prove it.

CHAPTER 3

"No body?" Matt Duncan, the elected District Attorney for King County asked Brunelle from across his desk. He pulled off his reading glasses to emphasize his incredulity. "You have no body?"

Brunelle frowned. That was the problem. "Afraid not," he admitted. "But I know she's dead."

"Uh-huh." Duncan set his glasses on his desk. "And how do you know that?"

"No one's seen her for three weeks now," Brunelle answered, but he knew the weakness of that response.

So did Duncan. "She was a hooker, right?"

"Prostitute," Brunelle quickly corrected. It seemed more respectful. He'd also heard the term 'sex worker,' but that seemed better applied to people who had some nominal choice in the matter. Maybe a high-priced call girl, or the regulated-and-taxed prostitutes in Europe. Not a drug-addicted, pimped-out, street-level prostitute picking up johns down near Occidental Park so she could eat that day. Still, no matter what label he attached to Amy, his answer was the same. "But, yes."

Duncan crossed his arms. "How do you know she didn't just

run away? Or went to another town? She could be hooking in Tacoma now. Or Portland. Or L.A. Maybe she went home to Iowa to visit her terminally ill grandmother."

Brunelle shook his head. He hadn't come to his boss's office completely unprepared. "No, she was born and raised in Seattle. Her mom and dad are local and her grandparents are dead. She lived in an apartment on Yesler, but she missed her rent payment, and none of her neighbors have seen her for three weeks."

Duncan frowned, and put his glasses earpiece in his mouth, but he didn't say anything back. It was a crack in his façade. Duncan was the boss because he was a damn good trial attorney, and an even better politician. But he was also the boss because he cared, passionately. About victims. And about justice.

"She's dead, Matt," Brunelle pressed his advantage. "I know it. And so do you. I know who killed her too. We can't just let him get away with it."

Duncan's frown deepened, joined by creases in his brow. He tapped his fingers on his desk for a few moments, then released the frown and sighed loudly. "Damn it, Dave. Do you have any idea what kind of circus this could turn into? I don't want to be answering questions about why we charged someone with murder if the jury is just going to acquit because we can't even prove she's dead."

Brunelle nodded. "I know, Matt. I know."

Duncan stood up and started pacing in front of the picture windows that looked out over downtown Seattle. Brunelle knew that meant he was thinking. Duncan was a thoughtful man. Brunelle felt grateful to work for him. He knew to stay quiet until Duncan was ready to share those thoughts.

But Brunelle could anticipate them.

Without turning around from the view of skyscrapers and

shipping vessels, Duncan asked the question Brunelle knew was the crux of it all. "Can you prove it?"

No body.

A victim who was drug-addicted and transient, in a dangerous occupation that involved getting into the cars of strange men.

A witness who'd been promised no one would ever know she'd spoken to the authorities.

A killer who was street-hardened, wasn't likely to be intimidated by police questioning, and commanded fear and loyalty from those who might have information against him.

Could he prove it? Brunelle didn't know. So he avoided the question and answered the more important one.

"I will."

CHAPTER 4

2628 S. 138th Street, SeaTac, Washington, 98168.

It had been easy enough for Brunelle to find Amy's most recent address. He knew not to look at her driver's license record—that was for the good, law-abiding people of the world, not drug-addicted, street-level prostitutes. They didn't stop by the DMV to update their addresses. No, he just looked up her last booking. It was only two months prior to her murder and included all the information he could possibly want: her real last-known address, phone number (likely disconnected already), height and weight (increasingly thinner every booking, thanks to the heroin or meth or whatever her latest vehicle of escape was), and even her tattoos (a butterfly on her ankle, Chinese characters on the nape of her neck, and the name 'Lydia' on her left forearm).

Probably her mom, Brunelle figured. *Or best friend from high school. Maybe even a girlfriend.* He'd heard a lot of prostitutes were actually lesbian in their romantic relationships. He could figure why. But, then again, he'd heard a lot of things.

But Amy's last-known address was some apartment on Yesler Street in Seattle that she probably shared with three or four other girls. Brunelle didn't want to visit them. Not in any capacity. He was looking for someone far more important. Not Amy; she was dead. Not her fellow prostitutes; they were as scared of Kenny as Linda was, some of them more so, no doubt. No, Brunelle was looking for the last time Amy's address didn't have an apartment number after the street name.

That's where he'd find her parents.

He pulled his rain-gray sedan to a stop across the street from the run-down rambler. Like all the other houses on the street, it was a one-story ranch, with moss on the roof and an overgrown lawn. A chain-link fence separated the yard from the busy road in front and the adjoining lots to either side, a 'Beware of Dog' sign hanging crookedly on the gate. Like in most of the Seattle suburbs, there was no sidewalk; the gate just opened up onto the shoulder of the roadway. Brunelle stepped out of his car and looked around for something pleasant to lift the mood of the place. But the sky was overcast, and the air was filled with that cold mist of a rain that most Seattleites don't even notice any more. He waited for a car to pass, then shoved his hands into his coat pockets and crossed the street.

The metal gate opened with a creak, and he made the short walk to the porch in just a few strides. The porch's wood was warped and weak-feeling. He opened the screen door enough to knock on the front door and stepped back to be visible through the peephole. As he waited for the door to open, he noticed absently that the '6' nailed to the peeling siding was more rusted than its address-number counterparts.

After a few moments, the front door opened with a thunk that shook the screen. It was dark inside, but Brunelle could see the face of the woman who hid most of herself behind the door. She was older than him, but probably not as old as she looked, with creased wrinkles and puffy eyes. His sentimental side suggested the eyes were puffy from crying. His cynical side guessed it was alcohol. His realist side knew it was both, and they were related.

"Mrs. Corrigan?" he started. "My name is David Brunelle. I'm a prosecutor with the King County Prosecutor's Office. I'd like to talk with you about Amy."

If he'd come a few weeks earlier, Mrs. Corrigan likely would have asked if Amy had been arrested again, or even more likely would have washed her hands of whatever trouble her daughter had gotten herself into again. But it wasn't a few weeks earlier, and Mrs. Corrigan knew something was wrong, even if she didn't exactly know—or wouldn't admit to herself—what it was.

"Is she okay?" the woman asked, opening the door enough to reveal a heavy-set frame in old clothes in front of an untidy living room lit only by a television screen.

Brunelle shook his head slightly. "No," he answered. "May I come in?"

Mrs. Corrigan hesitated only long enough to let Brunelle's response sink in, then she opened the door fully and stepped aside. She nodded at him to come inside, but couldn't quite find her voice. Brunelle opened the screen and walked into the home, overcoming his reluctance at both the setting and the circumstances.

The interior of the home held that level of unpleasantness that happens when the residents spent too much time there and had too few visitors. The shades were drawn, filtering even further what little light the Seattle sky allowed. There were old dinner plates and half-filled glasses on top of the magazines and newspapers that covered the coffee table. And there was a distinct smell of dog that was discernable even over the stench of cigarette smoke. He looked around and identified the least dirty-looking chair.

"May I sit down?" he asked.

"Of course, of course," Mrs. Corrigan replied, her voice returning to her, thanks to the distraction that small courtesies provide. "I'll go get Howard."

Brunelle nodded and sat down. He was glad both of Amy's parents were there. He didn't want to do this twice.

Howard was a reflection of his wife. He was overweight, most of it in his gut, with an irregularly balding hairline and tired jowls. His eyes held not the sadness of a fearful mother, but the hopelessness of a failed father. He held out a meaty hand. "I'm Howard Corrigan. Mary says you're from the prosecutor's office. She says you have some news about Amy."

Brunelle stood up to shake the man's hand. "I think I do," he answered. "But it's not good news. That's why I'm here."

Howard grimaced, but shrugged. He sat down on the couch, and his wife sat next to him, not even bothering to clear the cushion of the debris there. "We haven't heard from her for two weeks," Howard said. "We figured we'd hear from the cops soon, to identify the body."

Brunelle was struck by the resignation in Howard Corrigan's voice. He wasn't angry or scared. Just tired, exhausted by life.

"I didn't expect a prosecutor," Howard continued. "Do they send you guys now? Are you gonna take us to identify her body?"

Brunelle grimaced himself, then leaned forward and clasped his hands. "We don't have a body for you to identify," he admitted. "But I do think she's dead. In fact, I think she was murdered."

"Of course she was murdered," Howard suddenly snapped. "She wasn't gonna survive that lifestyle." Then his face turned from almost angry to almost puzzled. "Wait, how do you know she was murdered if you don't have her body?"

"That's why I'm here," Brunelle answered. "She's gone

missing, but her body hasn't been found. If I'm going to seek murder charges without a body, I need as much information as possible about what Amy would do if she were still alive."

Howard cocked his head askance. Mary added her own quizzical expression.

"If I can establish," Brunelle explained, "what she would do if she were alive, and then show that she's not doing it, that would be some evidence that she's not alive anymore."

The parents' expressions changed. Brunelle mistook it for incredulity.

"I know it's thin," he defended, "but it may be all I have. Can you think of anything significant that might have changed in the last few weeks?"

Mary shook her head. "It's not thin," she said.

"That's how we knew she was gone too," Howard confirmed.

It was Brunelle's turn to look confused. "I don't understand."

Mary smiled weakly then looked down the hallway toward the back of the house. "Lydia!" she called out. "Come here, honey."

Brunelle remembered the tattoo from Amy's booking info. "Who's Lydia?" he asked.

A two-year-old girl toddled into the living room, her hair in pigtails, her pink shirt dirty and stained. She didn't have any pants on over her diaper.

"Lydia is Amy's daughter," Mary introduced the child. "And she hasn't seen her mommy in two weeks."

"Amy might stop visiting her tired, old, nagging parents," Howard said, "but she'd never stop seeing her daughter. When she missed her weekly visit with Lydia, we knew something was wrong. When she missed the next one, well..." but he trailed off, unable to finish the thought aloud.

Mary scooped up Lydia and sat her on her large lap. "Can you do anything, Mr. Brunelle?" Mary asked. "Can you get justice for Lydia's mommy?"

Brunelle looked at the innocent young girl staring at him with wide, brown eyes. Then he swallowed the unexpected lump in his throat. "I can try."

CHAPTER 5

Brunelle pulled away from the house and switched on his windshield wipers against the misty drizzle that had developed while he was inside the Corrigans' home. He'd stayed longer than he'd wanted—or at least longer than he'd planned. Once he'd gotten what he needed—a reason he could feel confident Amy Corrigan was dead—he couldn't help but stay a bit longer and play dollies with that little reason. Lydia had jumped off her grandma's lap and run to fetch her favorite doll, a raggedy thing with pink yarn hair and a yellow dress.

Brunelle shook his head slightly and turned on his headlights, even though it was the middle of the afternoon. Ah, Seattle.

Why did he stay and play with some little girl he'd never met before? She wasn't *his* kid. He didn't have kids. If her own dad wasn't around, why should Brunelle care enough to play with Miss Flopsy-Curls or whatever the doll's name was? How could he possibly care about someone else's kid?

And, in his mind's eye, he suddenly saw the face of Lizzy Anderson, Kat's daughter.

Damn.

Yeah, how could he possibly care about someone else's kid?

Brunelle shook his head again and reached for his cell phone. He knew it was against Washington State law to talk on a cell phone while driving. He also knew the loophole in that law. He was a lawyer, after all. The drafters didn't want to outlaw the hands-free devices car companies were starting to put in their vehicles, so they only made it illegal if the driver spoke into a cell phone while holding it to his ear. So he just turned the volume up and held the phone in front of his mouth.

"Detective Chen."

"Larry, it's Brunelle," he said as he merged back onto I-5 north. "Do it."

There was a pause. A tired, pregnant pause. Finally, a sigh. Then, "Do what, Dave?"

"Arrest him."

"Arrest who?"

Brunelle could still see Lizzy's face in his mind, but it faded away as he remembered Lydia's huge brown eyes looking up innocently at this unknown man who'd been kind enough to play with her for even a few minutes.

"The pimp," Brunelle answered. "Kenny What's-his-name. Amy Corrigan's killer. Arrest him. I'm going to charge him with murder."

CHAPTER 6

Kenneth Wayne Brown.

Kenny the Pimp.

Murderer.

Brunelle watched through the same two-way mirror as before. Chen pushed Kenny into the plastic chair in the interrogation room and shut the door. It was gonna be two against one; Chen and fellow detective Julia Montero. Obviously, Kenny hated women, so no better way to antagonize him than to put a woman in a position of power over him. Piss him off. Because pissed-off people made bad decisions—like agreeing to talk to the police.

Brunelle knew he had nothing on Kenny. Or next to nothing. A missing prostitute, a suspicious friend, and a lonely toddler. That wasn't likely to add up to proof beyond a reasonable doubt. But despite the courts' best efforts in the half-century since *Miranda v. Arizona,* the vast majority of suspects still made statements even after the cops told them they probably shouldn't. People commit crimes because they calculate they can probably get away with it. It takes some time for that calculation to fade, even after an arrest.

People spend their lives talking their way out of things, whether with their parents, their teachers, or their significant others. The hubris we all succumb to sometimes leads suspects to think they can explain it all away, never realizing the only reason the cops want to bother talking to them is because they probably don't have enough evidence without the confession.

Kenny was a pimp. He made his living by convincing women to have sex with strangers and then give him all the money. Anybody who could do that could trick a couple of cops, right?

Of course, he couldn't punch the cops up for talking back to him. Brunelle allowed a small grin as the show started.

"You know why you're here, Kenneth," Montero started. It wasn't a question. It also wasn't the name he liked to use. 'Kenneth.' Like she was his mom, or his teacher. It was designed to irritate. Like a grain of sand inside an oyster. Hopefully, it would lead to the pearl of a confession.

"It's Kenny," he took the bait. Chen had undone his handcuffs, so he rubbed his wrists slightly as he replied. Then he smirked. "You're Julia, right?"

He could provoke too.

"That's Detective Montero," Chen leaned his large frame onto the small Formica table between him and his subject. "Show some respect."

But Montero eased her partner back into his seat with a gentle hand. "I can take care of myself, Larry."

Kenny's distasteful smile broadened. He looked her up and down. "I bet you can."

Montero was attractive enough, with long wavy brown hair and the athletic figure of a cop. But in her 30s, she was a little old for the streets. Brunelle knew half the prostitutes out there any more were in their early teens, well under the age of consent.

"Check yourself, Kenneth," she replied with her own grin. "I'm not some runaway looking for a roof and some food."

"See now," Kenny replied. "You get me. I just help those girls out. I'm a Good Samaritan."

"Good Samaritan?" Chen scoffed. "That's rich."

"Look, man." Kenny leaned back in his cheap plastic chair. "I don't find these girls, they find me. They're usually running from way worse than anything I could do to them. Abusive fathers, drunk mothers, horny uncles. I give them a place to live and a way to earn a living. That's why so many of them come to me."

"But you've got one less girl than you used to, huh, Kenny?" Chen narrowed his eyes at the pimp.

Kenny narrowed his own eyes. "Girls come and go, man."

Chen didn't reply right away. Moreno stepped into the breach. "You know that's not how it works, Kenny. And so do we."

Kenney didn't answer, but he did cross his arms. Discomfort.

"They come because you go get them," Moreno went on. "You find the runaways at the bus shelter, or the food bank, or just near some alley trying to score their next hit. You offer them a place to stay and some drugs. Food, too, if they care enough about eating. Then you introduce them to some of your more experienced girls who tell them there's a way they can make money. A lot of it. At first they're not sure, but they see all the money, and the other girls seem okay with it, so finally they agree. And you let them keep fifty percent—at first. That's a lot. A new girl can make five or six hundred bucks a day that way. That buys a lot of meth, or heroin, or whatever they're using. Both, probably. Maybe crack. But then you start demanding all of it. After all, you're paying for the hotel room. And you're the one who knows the dealers. You can kick them out any minute. Cut them off from their drugs and the roof over their heads."

Kenny frowned and shook his head. "They can leave whenever they want."

Moreno shook her head back at him. "Everybody knows that isn't true. The reason you found them in the first place is because they're runaways. The last place they want to go is back home. If they're gonna get molested by some disgusting drunk old man, at least it won't be their step-dad, or their uncle, or their drug-addicted mom's latest boyfriend."

Kenny shrugged and looked away. Translation: not my problem.

"Plus they'll get some money—at first. More than grandpa ever gave them for shoving his filthy fat hand down her pants. But then you start taking the money too. Some of them are smart enough and stay sober long enough to realize it's their ass they're selling, and they don't need you to sell it. They try to go solo, putting the same ads on the same websites, meeting up at the same no-questions-asked motels by I-5. But you're not gonna let that happen. If all the girls figure that out, you're out of business. And you're not gonna go out of business."

Kenny had turned back during Moreno's speech. He nodded at her and his grin returned. "I ain't in no business. Some ho wanna sell it on the streets, that ain't none of my business."

"That's exactly your business," Chen jumped in.

Brunelle grimaced. Chen wasn't a very good 'bad cop.' He was too nice a guy in reality. That made Brunelle smile again. Then he remembered that Chen was still mad at him. And why. And about who. His smile faded back into a frown, and he refocused on the exchange on the other side of the glass.

"Is that what happened to Amy?" Moreno asked. "Did she go renegade?"

Kenny seemed just barely taken aback by the question. Like he'd remembered something he'd wanted to forget. But he pulled his poker face back on in less than a moment. Or, more accurately, his pimp face.

"Renegade?" he repeated. "What are you, some kinda Old West sheriff or something?"

Moreno didn't take the bait. She was way too experienced to be distracted by some perp.

"Renegade is your word, Kenneth," she replied. "I've done enough of these cases. We get warrants for your phones, read all your texts. 'Bitch gone renegade,'" she quoted in a deeper, mock pimp voice. "'Gonna teach that ho a lesson.' Next thing she knows, your fist is in her eye and her ass is back in your room."

Kenny's expression hardened, but he didn't say anything. Brunelle figured he was wondering whether they'd already gotten all his text messages, and was trying to remember what he'd said in them. Anything about Amy?

"So I'll ask you again," Moreno leaned on to the table. "Is that what happened to Amy?"

It was another decision point for Kenny the Pimp. He should have started the interview with a simple, 'Fuck you. I want a lawyer.' But he didn't. He thought he could outsmart the detectives. He had his story set for an interrogation about pimping. He offered girls room and board, and they were generous enough to repay him. How they earned their money was their own business.

But murder? That was a different matter. Of course, the only reason Kenny would know it was murder was because he'd murdered her. Lawyering up at this point would make him look guilty as hell. Brunelle knew they could never tell the jury that he'd lawyered up. They'd just pretend the interview ended right before the question about Amy. Brunelle knew that detail of criminal procedure. But Kenny didn't. So he screwed up again. Police work relied heavily on the mistakes of the criminals.

"Amy who?" he tried. "I don't know no Amy."

Time for a bluff. They hadn't gotten his phone. Hell, they weren't even sure the prosecutors would take the case. Brunelle called and said arrest him. All they had was the phone from Kenny's pocket. It probably had incriminating texts on it, but it would take a warrant—probably more than one—to do a full forensic examination on the phone. They had his texts, they just hadn't read them yet. But he didn't know that.

"We have your texts, Kenny," Chen practically growled.

It was a big gamble. The suggestion was that the detectives knew damn well Kenny knew who Amy was. But if Kenny knew he hadn't texted about her, then he would know they were full of shit. The good news was that everyone—even pimps—texted like crazy any more. And no one—not even pimps—could remember all of their texts.

After several long seconds of glaring, Kenny gave a far too exaggerated shrug and looked away again. "Yeah, okay, maybe I know an Amy. Shit, I know a lot of girls."

Moreno nodded. "I'm sure you do. But how many do you know that have been murdered?"

Kenny snapped back to stare right into Moreno's eyes. He held her gaze for several seconds. Then he growled too. "More than you, bitch."

Brunelle was impressed by the force of Kenny's reply. Chen, apparently, less so.

"Oh, poor fucking baby," he said. "You've had a rough life, is that it? Lost a lot of loved ones to the mean streets of Seattle, huh? Well, suck it up, punk. I've stood over more dead bodies than you, and I'll stand over a lot more before I'm done putting scum like you behind bars."

Okay, that was a pretty good bad cop, Brunelle had to admit.

But Kenny smiled despite the barrage. He locked eyes with Chen this time. "But you ain't stood over Amy's body, have you?"

"Fuck," Brunelle exhaled.

He knew the cops shared his sentiment. They couldn't say, 'No,' because that would give away that they didn't have anything. But they couldn't say, 'Yes,' either. Not because they weren't allowed to lie to a suspect—they did that all the time. But because the suspect would know they were lying.

So Moreno tried to deflect. "We know you killed her, Kenny."

Kenny pursed his lips and grabbed his chin. He looked the two detectives up and down. Then nodded. "You don't know shit," he realized. So he went ahead and told a story he knew they couldn't refute. "I ain't seen Amy for a month. I don't know shit about where she is. And that's all I got to say about it."

Chen's hands balled into fists. Moreno's jaw tensed and she sat back in her chair.

"You got anything to say about it?" Kenny taunted.

"Yeah." Chen stood up sharply and sent his own plastic chair slamming into the wall behind him. "You're under arrest for the murder of Amy Corrigan."

CHAPTER 7

The arrest was on a Tuesday. That meant the arraignment would be Wednesday. By court rule—and Constitutional mandate—everyone arrested for a crime had to be brought before a judge by the next day, even on weekends. The judge would determine if there was 'probable cause' for the arrest and, if so, set some sort of bail.

By the same court rules, Brunelle could have asked for the suspect to be held for an additional 48 hours while the investigation continued and additional evidence was gathered. That happened a lot when a suspect was caught fleeing the scene, but the cops were still doing their jobs—especially if forensic tests were needed to identify the perpetrator. But for Amy's murder, Brunelle figured, *Why bother?* The case wasn't going to get any better.

Brunelle made his way down to the arraignment courtroom, the file under his arm, and the charging paperwork inside the file. Washington State didn't use grand juries; the decision to charge a person with a crime was vested in the prosecutor alone. It was more efficient, but there was no one to hide behind.

With great power comes great blame.

As he walked through the gallery, Brunelle avoided the cameramen and reporters, apart from an obligatory greeting nod. There was no way he was going to give a sound bite on this one. Not before the arraignment anyway. Probably not before the trial either. *Maybe* after the verdict. *If* he got a conviction.

He passed through the secure door into the glassed-off front section of the courtroom, separated from the general public so the jailors could bring the inmates directly into the courtroom via an interior corridor from the jail, without any of the risks associated with marching handcuffed criminals through the hallways of a public courthouse. It made for a cozy, almost clubhouse like feel for the lawyers. His adversary, and friend, Jessica Edwards was waiting for him inside the clubhouse.

"Good morning, Dave," she greeted him as she extended her hand. But not for a handshake. "Do you have the charging docs?"

Brunelle reached into his file and handed her two copies of the 'information.' Seattle was a nice city—'To your face anyway,' as a colleague from the East Coast once remarked—so prosecutors didn't file 'complaints.' 'Complaint' was a mean word. It suggested the defendant had done something wrong, and that might hurt the defendant's feelings. No, in Washington, the formal pleading that charged a person with committing a crime was called an 'information'—because it 'informed' the defendant of the charges. Just in case he wanted to know why the mean ol' prosecutors were trying to put him prison.

Attached to the information was a summary of the facts supporting the charge. It was called the 'declaration for the determination of probable cause.' Judges read it to make sure there were at least some facts to support the charges. Again, a pretty low standard, but one that had to be met before a judge could impose bail or other release conditions.

Lawyers used it too. It was a lot easier to read a two- or three-page summary of a case than wade through hundreds, or even thousands, of pages of police reports. Those few pages let the lawyers know what evidence the state had. And what they didn't.

Edwards finished reading it and looked up at Brunelle, her expression an amalgam of surprise, curiosity, excitement, and hope. "You don't have the body?"

"I don't need the body," Brunelle shot back, a little too quickly to sound as confident as his words tried to be.

Edwards raised her palms defensively. "Hey, no complaints, Dave. I'm happy to defend a murder case where you can't even prove anyone is actually dead."

Brunelle crossed his arms. Another failure to project confidence. "It's called circumstantial evidence."

"It's called an acquittal," Edwards muttered, only half to herself. Then, raising her voice again. "When I saw that you'd filed charges, I just figured you must have found the body."

Brunelle's already fixed frown deepened, but his demeanor lightened a bit. He couldn't stay irritated at her. She was just pointing out the truth. "Nope." With some effort he replaced the frown with a practiced smile. "It'll just be that much more satisfying when the jury says, 'guilty as charged.'"

Edwards smiled too, but hers was genuine—and just as challenging. "You have to get in front of a jury first, Dave. No body means the first thing I'm going to do is file a motion to dismiss for lack of *corpus delicti*. You can't even show a murder has actually happened, let alone that my client did it."

Brunelle shrugged. "I figured as much. I'll be ready for that motion. There's case law that a case can proceed without a body."

That was true, but the reason there was case law decided by the appellate courts was because several trial courts had been willing to dismiss bodyless cases, thus leading to the appeal in the first place. He made a mental note to call Chen and urge him to keep looking for the body even though he'd gone ahead and filed charges. Then he made another mental note to figure out some way to get Chen to stop being mad at him. Detectives who are colleagues do their jobs. Detectives who are friends do favors.

"All rise!" The bailiff announced the arrival of the judge before Brunelle could make any more mental notes. He turned to see who was walking out from chambers. The arraignment judge varied day to day, depending on who had other things to do and who could stand to spend all day doing nothing but reading charges and hearing defense attorneys say, 'My client pleads not guilty, Your Honor.' Some of the judges liked it—a nice break from trial work—but most of them didn't. Who the judge was didn't always matter, but it did when there were close calls. This was a little closer of a call than Brunelle normally liked, so who the judge was might matter after all.

It was Brian Jackson.

Brunelle nodded slightly to himself. Jackson was fine, nothing special. Your typical late-50s male, appointed by the governor a few years earlier when one of the older judges retired. He'd distinguished himself by being undistinguishing. Average appearance—thinning hair and widening waistline—and predictable rulings. He usually ruled the right way and managed not to piss off either the prosecutor's office or the defense bar. Not yet anyway.

But there was always time for that.

Jackson told everyone to be seated, then followed suit himself. He looked down at the junior prosecutor who played *maître d'* for the day's docket of arraignments and bail hearings. "Which matter is ready first, Miss Santos?"

Santos acknowledged the judge with a professional nod. "Mr. Brunelle has a matter ready," she replied. She stepped aside to give her superior a spot at the bar. "The Kenneth Brown arraignment."

Brunelle stepped forward, his frown threatening to return. It was already happening. 'The Kenneth Brown case.' Not 'the Amy Corrigan case.' Even his own prosecutor was doing it.

"This is the Amy Corrigan murder," Brunelle announced as he handed the charging paperwork forward to Judge Jackson's clerk.

Edwards stepped to the bar as well and let out a faint, yet somehow professional, scoff. "Maybe."

Jackson raised an eyebrow at her, but didn't say anything. Instead, he began reading the paperwork even as the jailor escorted Kenny Brown into the courtroom. He'd been booked on murder, with no chance to post bail until he'd been seen in open court. Despite the orange jail-jammies, plastic sandals, and handcuffs attached to belly chains, he somehow managed to saunter into the courtroom, as cocky as ever.

"Hello, Kenny," Brunelle heard Edwards whisper to her client. "Just let me do the talking. I think this will go well."

Before Brunelle could think of a comeback—let alone whether he should make one to an eavesdropped comment between attorney and client—Judge Jackson looked up from the pleadings. "There's no body?" That eyebrow was now aimed squarely at Brunelle.

But Brunelle was ready—he hadn't wasted his best line of his pre-arraignment banter with Edwards. "Oh, there's a body," he answered the judge. "It just hasn't been recovered yet."

Jackson's eyebrow hesitated for a moment, then relaxed. Brunelle's comment was sound-bitey, but it carried a point. Jackson looked to the defense. "Ms. Edwards, have you received copies of the information?"

"Yes, Your Honor," Edwards replied. "We acknowledge receipt, waive formal reading, and enter a plea of not guilty." Then the important part. "Before the court hears argument on conditions of release, we'd like to be heard on the issue of probable cause. We believe the court should find there are insufficient facts to find probable cause and immediately release my client."

Brunelle had anticipated that too.

Jackson looked to Brunelle. "The facts *are* pretty thin, Mr. Brunelle," he said. "Do you think I can find probable cause without a body?"

Brunelle nodded. "You can and you should. As I mentioned to defense counsel prior to Your Honor taking the bench, there is ample case law supporting verdicts of murder when no body is recovered. If a jury can find murder beyond a reasonable doubt without a body, then an arraignment court can certainly find probable cause. We'd ask you to do so and then set bail."

"Those cases are distinguishable," Edwards was ready, too, with her reply. "The facts in those cases are very different from what we have here. A woman reported missing by her coworkers but not her husband, blood found in the residence, and no reason to expect the victim simply ran away. But in this case, the alleged victim led a very transient and dangerous lifestyle. The fact that she hasn't been seen for a few weeks hardly supports the inference that she's dead, let alone that she was murdered—and let alone by my client. The court should decline to find probable cause and release my client unconditionally."

Under the law, even if a judge found no probable case, the state could still proceed with the prosecution. It was pretty rare, if only because there was usually more than enough evidence to find probable cause; the state wasn't supposed to go around charging citizens with crimes without evidence. The real problem was that if a judge didn't find probable cause, he couldn't set bail—Brown would walk out the door without posting a dime.

Jackson looked back to Brunelle. "Any reply?"

Brunelle gave a small shrug. He tried to take on the demeanor of 'reasonable prosecutor.' The state wasn't supposed to file charges without evidence, *ergo* since charges had been filed, there must be evidence. "The state believes there is sufficient evidence for the court to find probable cause and we ask you to do so. We're then prepared to argue conditions of release."

Jackson chewed his cheek, but only for a moment. He understood that his main job was to make decisions. "Probable cause is a very low standard," he said. "The lowest, in fact. Basically, are there facts sufficient to support the inference of the charges? I have my doubts about whether there's enough evidence to convict the defendant beyond a reasonable doubt, but that's not what I'm being asked to decide. I'm being asked to decide if there are facts to support the charge, and I'm going to find that there are."

Brunelle breathed a sigh of relief. A glance to his right showed Brown was disappointed.

Edwards was nonplussed. "Thank you, Your Honor," she said. "We'd ask for a personal recognizance release."

Even Brunelle was surprised by the boldness of that request. P.R. on a murder? Murderers didn't get P.R.ed.

Jackson's eyebrow raised again, but not as high as before. "A P.R.?" he confirmed.

"Yes, Your Honor," Edwards replied. "The court has found the facts, as thin as they are, support probable cause, but they do not support holding my client in custody while the state flails about, hoping to find a body before the trial date. My client is presumed innocent and should be treated accordingly."

Jackson nodded at the argument and turned to Brunelle. "Reply?"

Brunelle hadn't thought Edwards would be bold enough to ask for a P.R., although he supposed he should have. He'd have to remember, friendly banter or not, she was going to do her best for her client.

"The defendant is charged with murder in the first degree," Brunelle replied matter-of-factly. "The court has found probable cause for the charge. Bail for that charge is typically one million dollars. We'd ask the court to set bail at one million, along with standard conditions of no contact with prospective witnesses, avoiding the crime scene, and remaining in contact with his defense attorney."

Jackson cocked his head. "I can't order him to stay away from the crime scene, Mr. Brunelle. No one knows where that is."

Brunelle didn't have a reply ready for that either; but, then again, Jackson's tone didn't invite any response.

"I also can't set bail at one million dollars," Jackson continued. "I may have found probable cause, but Ms. Edwards is correct. Her client is presumed innocent, and the evidence in this case is far less than in the typical case."

Damn, Brunelle thought.

"But neither can I simply release Mr. Brown on his own recognizance. The charges are serious, and the facts presented, such as they are, suggest that there is a risk Mr. Brown may not return to court without some surety."

It was Edwards' turn to frown.

"Therefore," Jackson concluded, "I'm going to set bail in the amount of one hundred thousand dollars. If the defendant posts bail, then I will order him to have no contact with prospective witnesses, and that he keep in contact with Ms. Edwards."

Again Judge Jackson threaded the needle. Neither side could say he'd totally screwed them. But Brunelle was far more screwed than Edwards. $100,000 was nothing. Brown would only have to come up with $10,000 to pay a bonding company to post the full 100K for him. He was a pimp and a drug dealer. He probably had $10,000 in his bedside table. He'd call one of his girls and be out by dinnertime.

Brunelle nodded anyway. "Thank you, Your Honor."

The hearing was over. For Brunelle, as a lawyer who would be going home that night to a safe apartment and Chinese take-out, it was probably a draw.

But for the witnesses Brown was no doubt about to start intimidating, it was a definite loss.

CHAPTER 8

"Larry, it's Brunelle. I need your help."

Brunelle could hear Chen suppress a groan over the telephone. He had to wait several seconds for Chen to actually say anything. And then it wasn't what he'd hoped for. More like what he'd expected.

"Dave," Chen practically sighed. "Look, I'm, uh, kinda busy right now."

The fact that Chen was sitting at his desk and actually answering his phone meant Chen was anything but busy right then.

"Don't worry, Larry," Brunelle replied, his previous trepidation at calling his friend starting to melt away. The judgmental friend bit was growing tiresome. "This'll be quick. The judge set Brown's bail at a hundred-K. He'll be out by nightfall. We need to get some protection for Linda."

And by 'we,' Brunelle, of course, meant 'you.' Brunelle wasn't a cop. He didn't go around carrying a gun and talking to prostitutes. That's was Chen's job.

But Chen apparently disagreed. "I'm a detective, Dave, not a bodyguard."

Brunelle twisted his mouth into a tight frown. One of the advantages of telephone conversations was that the other party couldn't see your facial expressions. That could also be a disadvantage when you wanted to communicate the fact that the other person was being a real jerk.

"You're supposed to serve and protect," Brunelle countered. "Linda needs protection."

There was no pause this time. And no maudlin sigh. They were moving past that, apparently. "Don't lecture me, Dave. I know damn well what my job is, and I know damn well I don't need advice from you. You stick to filing papers and fucking defense attorneys."

Ah.

"Is that what this is all about?" Brunelle asked. "You're mad at me because I had a relationship with someone on the other side?"

"Relationship?" Chen scoffed. "You fucked her. Big deal. And I couldn't care less what team she's on. But when you fucked her, you fucked over someone who really cares about you."

One of the pieces of advice Brunelle always gave young prosecutors was to never let the other side get you angry; when you get angry, you make mistakes; you say things you shouldn't.

Do as I say, not as I do.

"You don't know shit about my relationship with Robyn," Brunelle growled. As much as he'd tried not to think about Kat's feelings for him, he'd been trying even harder not to think about his feelings for Robyn. He redirected that pain into aggression at his friend. "Or my relationship with Kat, for that matter. You went out to dinner with us once or twice. Fine. Great. I'll call you if I need to remember her favorite dish. But you weren't around for all of it and you, of all people, should know people aren't always what they seem."

"*You* sure aren't," Chen chided. "I thought you were a good man."

Brunelle ignored the *ad hominem* attack. Instead, he countered with, "And I thought you cared about the people you're supposed to protect."

"Like Linda Prescott?" Chen asked. "You want me to protect her? Dave, you don't have the first idea how to protect her. You think she's safer if some cop comes around to talk to her and doesn't arrest her? Pulls her aside to whisper in her ear while all the other girls watch? You think that will make her safer? Don't be an idiot, Dave. They'll rat her out to her pimp faster than they make a nervous john cum."

Brunelle hesitated. He hadn't thought of that.

"Leave the police work to the police, Dave," Chen admonished. "I don't tell you how to try a case. Don't tell me how to serve and protect."

Brunelle nodded, but, again, only for himself. "Fine."

"But let me ask you a question," Chen said.

Brunelle paused, clenching his jaw. He wasn't in the mood for questions, or the advice that usually followed that kind of set up. "Sure," he growled.

"Why do you care so much about some stranger, but not about someone who actually cares about you too?"

Brunelle didn't say anything for several moments. His expression, had Chen been able to see it, was a stony poker face.

"Goodbye, Larry."

He hung up before Chen could echo the sentiment.

CHAPTER 9

Brunelle sat at his desk and stewed for way too long after hanging up with Chen. But he couldn't escape the fact that the detective had a point. Not about Kat—Chen could stay the hell out of Brunelle's love life. About Linda. She wouldn't be safer if some uniformed cop came and visited her on her street corner. But Brunelle wasn't a cop and his uniform made him look like every other businessman looking for a quick lay.

Like most of his knowledge about the criminal underworld, Brunelle had to rely on the police reports to tell him where to find Linda. He'd never even considered going to a prostitute. Apart from the moral repugnance of perpetuating the victimization of women so desperate they sell their bodies to strangers to fund their pimps' lavish lifestyles, he just never found it appealing. If he was going to have sex with someone, he wanted it be with someone who wanted to have sex with him too, not just someone who got paid to pretend. He didn't understand how any man could find that arousing enough to actually perform.

But looking at the foot traffic on Aurora Avenue, there was no shortage of men looking to spend their money on women like

Linda Prescott.

Brunelle shook his head and felt renewed irritation at Chen. There he was, cruising a strip of motels that everyone in Seattle knew was a hotbed of prostitution activity. Why couldn't the cops clean it up? Any given night, they could make two dozen arrests without breaking a sweat. Why not try to make a dent in it?

But he knew the answer. Working as a prostitute was only a misdemeanor; so was going to a prostitute. The johns might get embarrassed, but they weren't going to get any jail time. The women weren't going to get any jail time, either—not more than a few days, which was probably better than living on the streets anyway—so they weren't about to testify against their pimps, the only people worth going after. Since the pimps were never directly involved in the transaction, there was no way to prosecute them without the women's cooperation. So it all falls down like a house of cards and the good people of the world just look away as they drive over the Aurora Bridge toward downtown with their dinner reservations and opera tickets.

Luckily, Brunelle didn't have anybody to take to the opera.

But he was looking for a 'date.'

Aurora Avenue was the name the city fathers put on the part of the old Pacific Highway that ran north of downtown. It was three lanes in each direction, with a concrete barrier down the middle and no stoplights for miles. Not exactly the best place for slowing down to chat up a prostitute, but there were a half-dozen cheap, no-questions-asked motels clustered there; so what it lacked in accommodation for the front half of the transaction, it more than made up for on the back end.

For Brunelle, though, it made it difficult to just scan for Linda Prescott. It was already going to be difficult to find a woman he'd seen one time, weeks ago, in the dark and streetlights of late-night Seattle. But to make matters worse, he couldn't just slow down and take a look at who might be walking the streets. Instead, he had to do what the other perverts were doing: pulling into parking lots and waiting for the girls to approach their cars, offering a 'date' and, quite literally, a pricelist.

He sped past the area his first time through, so he had to turn around a few miles north and head back. When he got back, he slowed and pulled into the parking lot of the Aurora Motel, the one with the biggest sign on the strip.

"Size doesn't matter," he quipped to himself—but only to fight off the anxiety rising in his chest as he waded into what was going to look increasingly like criminal activity, and embarrassing criminal activity at that.

There were several women—and, Brunelle knew, girls—milling about near the driveway. None of them looked like Linda. Then again, none of them probably looked like themselves at all. Thick eyeliner, excessive lipstick, and overdone hair disguised each of them from whoever they really were. A safety mechanism for themselves and the johns. It wasn't about people; it was just about sex.

"Hey, there," said a woman who'd broken from the herd and was walking up to Brunelle's car. His hands suddenly started sweating. "Looking for a date?"

It wasn't Linda. He could tell that much even when she was a few feet away. Wrong hair color, wrong skin color, wrong height.

"Uh, maybe," he stammered. "I'm kinda looking for someone in particular."

The prostitute leaned onto his car door, her perfume assaulting him through the open window. It was floral and sickening at the same time. "Tell me who you're looking for, honey. I bet I can be her."

Brunelle shook his head. "No. It's not like that. I mean..."

But he stopped himself. He looked again at the woman leaning on his car. He had no idea who she was. He didn't know who her pimp was. He didn't know if she'd help Linda or turn her in. He craned his neck and looked at the other prostitutes still milling about at the driveway entrance. He didn't know any of them. He didn't know what any of them would do.

And, he realized, he didn't know what the hell he was doing, either.

"What's it like, honey?" the woman asked. "You somebody's regular?" She stepped back to look more carefully at him. "I ain't seen you before."

And now he was drawing attention to himself.

He could hear Chen's voice. *You think she's safer if some cop comes around to talk to her and doesn't arrest her? Don't be an idiot, Dave. They'll rat her out to her pimp faster than they make a nervous john cum.*

"Uh, yeah, well..." Brunelle spluttered.

"You a cop or something?" the woman asked, taking a step back.

Worse, Brunelle thought. *Prosecutor.*

But before he could figure out a polite way to end the conversation and get the hell out of there—and with a faint awareness of how ridiculous it was that he cared about being polite—one of the other women shouted over to them.

"Hey, Kelly! Watch out! The cops are here!"

At first Brunelle thought he was being further pegged as a cop, but when he turned around to look at the group, he could see two Seattle PD patrol cars on the other side of Aurora, pulling into another motel parking lot, their lights flashing red and blue across the highway.

Kelly—if that was even her real name—didn't give a shit about being polite and bolted from Brunelle's car window. He watched, almost detached, as she and the other women scurried into the three or four motel rooms Brunelle knew their pimp had rented—with the money they'd earned.

Brunelle relaxed in the presence of law enforcement and decided it was time he got the heck out of there. As he pulled back onto Aurora and headed for the Space Needle, Brunelle had to smile despite the abject failure of his mission. Maybe Chen and Company were trying to make a dent in the problem after all.

But the smile faded as he reached the south end of the Aurora Bridge, the patrol cars' lights long gone behind him. Maybe those cops were spontaneously arresting a handful of johns and prostitutes. Maybe.

Or maybe they'd been called out to a report of another murdered prostitute.

CHAPTER 10

Brunelle decided not to call Chen. Not because he didn't want Chen's help. He just didn't want to hear him say, 'Told you so.'

But he still needed information.

"Montero. Major Crimes." It was a simple way to answer a phone, but very impressive. He might have to try that. 'Brunelle. Homicides.' Yeah, that sounded good.

"Hey, Detective Montero," Brunelle greeted. "It's Dave Brunelle from the prosecutor's office. Do you have a few minutes?"

"Sure thing," Montero replied. "I'm just doing paperwork. Any break from that is a good thing. What can I do for you?"

Brunelle smiled. It was nice to talk to a friendly cop again. He was going to have to figure out some way to bury the hatchet with Chen.

Or maybe he could just start calling Julia Montero for help.

"It's about the Amy Corrigan murder," Brunelle started. "I had a question about Linda Prescott."

"Corrigan... Corrigan..." Montero repeated. "Oh, yeah. You mean the Kenny Brown case, right?"

Brunelle sighed. "Right."

"So what do you need?" Montero asked. "And who's Linda Prescott?"

Brunelle was surprised for a moment, then remembered Montero had been in on their interrogation of Kenny Brown, but not the interview of Linda Prescott.

"Uh…" Brunelle hesitated. The whole point of calling Montero was to avoid involving Chen. But if Montero didn't even know who Linda was, she'd just end up walking down the hall to relay any of Brunelle's questions anyway.

So, different tack. "Uh, were there any murders on Aurora Ave last night?"

Montero thought for a moment. "We didn't have any homicides at all last night."

That was good news. Brunelle was quiet for a moment as he considered the implications. Why were those cop cars there? Was it really just a bust of a few johns and hookers?

"What's going on, Mr. Brunelle?" Montero asked. "Does somebody need our help?"

Brunelle thought for a moment before replying. Someone did need help. But Chen was right too: Brunelle couldn't protect Linda Prescott on the mean streets of Seattle. He wasn't a cop; he was a lawyer.

He couldn't protect her on the streets. But maybe he could do it the courtroom.

CHAPTER 11

Brunelle walked up to his legal assistant's desk. "Have you sent out the police reports on the Amy Corrigan case yet, Nicole?"

Nicole looked up from the stack of paper she was collating. "Which case?"

Brunelle suppressed an eye roll. "Kenneth Brown. The Kenneth Brown case. Did you send the police report to defense counsel yet?"

"Oh, that case," Nicole replied. She patted the two-inch thick stack of paper on her desk. "I was just about to."

"Good," Brunelle said. Then he extended a hand. "I need to go through it first."

Nicole's expression betrayed some curiosity, but it was overcome by the opportunity to get some work off her desk. She handed the reports to Brunelle. "Need to add something?" she asked.

Brunelle tucked the reports under his arm and plucked a Sharpie off Nicole's desk. "Just the opposite."

* * *

"You have one witness who saw the victim with my client

just before she disappeared," Jessica Edwards said as Brunelle walked up to her in the Pit, the place where the attorneys negotiated cases at the pre-trial conference, "and you blacked out her name."

Brunelle smiled smugly as he sat down next to her. "How do you know it's a 'her'?"

Edwards tapped her binder of police reports. "Because it's pretty obvious from the interview that it's one of his prostitutes."

"There are male prostitutes," Brunelle pointed out.

"Not that work for my client," Edwards retorted.

"So he admits he's a pimp?" Brunelle asked.

"Of course he's a pimp," Edwards snapped. "But he's not a murderer. And anyway, you can't prove either crime without your mystery witness, so you can't hide her identity from me."

Brunelle crossed his arms and leaned back in his chair. "Ever heard of a confidential informant?"

Edwards uncrossed hers and leaned forward. "Ever heard of the Confrontation Clause?"

Brunelle waved the comment away. "That's a trial right. If this goes to trial, then you can confront her on the stand." He thought for a moment, then grinned, "or *him*."

"Of course it's going to trial," Edwards replied. "He's charged with murder. and you don't have a body. You don't expect me to plead him out to that, do you?"

"Why not?" Brunelle replied. "He's guilty."

"Not if you can't prove it beyond a reasonable doubt."

There were several dozen attorneys in the Pit, a roughly 50/50 split of prosecutors and defense attorneys. They all had their own cases and conversations to have, but heads were starting to turn as Brunelle and Edwards' conversation heated up.

"Whether I can prove something beyond a reasonable doubt," Brunelle posited, "is pretty much irrelevant to whether it actually happened. He either did it or he didn't."

"Whether he actually did it or not," Edwards replied, "is a separate question from whether you can prove it. And equally irrelevant. You shouldn't be able to prove it if he didn't do it, but even if he did, you still might not be able to prove it. And that's all that matters."

"It doesn't matter if he's guilty?" Brunelle scoffed.

"It matters if you can prove he's guilty beyond a reasonable doubt," was Edwards reply. "I don't give a shit if he did it or not. I care if you have the evidence to prove it in a court of law."

"Wait. You don't care that he murdered someone?" Brunelle clarified. "You don't care at all that a woman is dead now because your client killed her?"

"What I care about is defending my client against the charges filed against him." Edwards sat up straight in her chair, like an affronted mother. "I have an absolute ethical duty to defend him to the best of my ability. If that means an acquittal because you don't have the evidence to convict him, then so be it."

Brunelle shook his head. "That's wrong."

"No." Edwards pointed a finger at him. "That's justice."

Pretty much every other attorney had stopped their own conversation to listen in on Brunelle and Edwards. The two of them had almost fifty years of combined experience in criminal law and had tried some of the biggest cases of the last decade. Clash of the Titans.

"So you're telling me," Brunelle challenged, "that you would defend the case exactly the same regardless of whether your client told you he was with his sick grandma all night or he drew you a map of where he buried the body."

"What my client tells me is absolutely privileged." Edwards somehow managed to appear even more offended.

"Right." Brunelle rolled his eyes. "I remember learning something about that in law school. But that's not really my point. My point is that you already have better information than me. Your client knows he killed Amy Corrigan and he knows where he dumped the body. He probably also knows which of his girls is most likely to rat him out. So just because I black out a name to try to protect someone from your obviously murderous client doesn't really impact your ability to defend him because you already know more than me anyway."

Edwards took a deep breath, then a smile cracked her visage. "First of all, nice try. But I'm not going to tell you what my client said to me. Second, what he said is irrelevant. It doesn't matter what I know. It matters what you can prove, and how. And if you're going to call 'confidential hooker number one' as a witness, then I get her name and contact information before trial and I get to interview her before trial. The Confrontation Clause is meaningless if I'm not fully prepared to cross examine her when she takes the stand at trial."

Brunelle wasn't completely convinced Edwards had the moral high ground, but he knew the case law supported her. Still, he wasn't about to just throw Linda Prescott under the pimp-mobile.

"So file a motion to compel," he challenged. "And we'll see if the judge agrees with you."

Edwards' smile hardened but didn't fade. "Don't worry, Dave. I will."

CHAPTER 12

Edwards' brief was excellent. Of course. Brunelle hadn't really expected any less. There was a reason she was one of the top attorneys at the public defender's office. It still pissed Brunelle off that a pimp could bail himself out of jail with $10,000 cash, then claim poverty and get a public defender, because all of his money was illegal and therefore unreportable. But that was how the system worked.

The other way the system worked was that Brunelle was tasked with representing the public and upholding justice, but it was the damn defense attorneys who always got to cite the Constitution in their briefs.

The Sixth Amendment says, 'In all criminal prosecutions, the accused shall enjoy the right to be confronted with the witnesses against him.' The courts have interpreted that to mean more than simply getting to see them in open court, but to have a meaningful opportunity for effective cross examination. Just like Edwards said in the Pit.

There was a thin line of case law supporting keeping witnesses' identity secret, but the cases mostly dealt with the early stages of the case, not trial and trial preparation. Still, it was all he could find, so he built a brief around it and hit 'Save' one last time at 5:49 the night before his response was due. He'd proofread it in the morning.

It was time for a drink.

'Whither' was a restaurant and bar on the west side of Capitol Hill, past Broadway but not quite to Madison Park. It featured cheap mixed drinks and garlic kale. Brunelle didn't eat kale, but he didn't mind a drinking glass full of five different liquors for only eight bucks. Or two glasses full. By the time he finished the second glass, he was almost buzzed enough to try some kale after all, but not so far gone that he didn't know to stop after two drinks. So he had to kill an hour until his blood alcohol level was low enough to drive home.

He kept the tab open in case he ordered the kale after all, but switched to ice water and decided to pass the time people-watching from his spot at the bar. The place was full, mostly couples and double dates judging by the almost perfect one man/one woman ratio. 'Almost,' because he was there very alone.

The distraction was entertaining at first. Moving his gaze from one table to another, trying to discern the status of each group.

Was that couple on a first date? Was it their last?

Was that group of four really two couples? Or was it just four friends sharing a drink?

Was that guy already drunk?

Was that Robyn Dunn?

Brunelle's heart raced at the possible sight of his former paramour. He couldn't be sure from that distance, in that light, at that angle. But there was definitely a young woman with soft reddish curls facing away from him and talking to an enragingly good-looking young man.

The good-looking part was enraging, but so was the young part. He hadn't forgotten how much younger Robyn was than him. He also hadn't forgotten those curls, or how they felt in his hand when he held her. His heart sank at the thought of her out with another man. Especially that man. That good-looking young man.

"Another drink?" the bartender asked. Brunelle ripped his gaze away from the woman across the room and looked to the woman taking his drink orders. She was nice enough to look at too, although perhaps a little heavier than he usually preferred. Still, she had a pretty face with brown curls of her own, and soft eyes that peered over small, stylish glasses. For a moment, he wondered whether the lenses even had a prescription or were just for looks, but then he remembered it was Seattle. Everyone was nearsighted and vitamin D deficient.

"Uh, no thanks," he replied, and held up his water glass. "I'm just waiting until I'm okay to drive."

"Do you want anything else?" she asked.

Brunelle looked back over to the table with the red-haired girl and the good-looking young man. This time, the woman turned enough for Brunelle to see her profile—it wasn't Robyn after all. Just another beautiful young woman he had no business thinking about.

Brunelle shook his head, in part as a response to the bartender's question, in part to shake out thoughts of young redheads and curvaceous brunettes. "No, thanks." He pulled out his wallet and handed her a credit card. "In fact, I think I'm ready to go home after all. I'll just call a cab." He looked over at not-Robyn again and sighed. "I have a big day tomorrow."

CHAPTER 13

Brunelle wasn't lucky enough to draw Judge Jackson again for Edwards' motion to compel the name of his confidential witness. Not that Jackson was on Brunelle's all-star judge list after setting bail so low on Brown, but at least he'd found probable cause. Brunelle would have had a shot with Jackson. Not so with the judge they were assigned to: Judge Helen Grissom.

Grissom had no love for law enforcement, and in her view the prosecutors were just an extension of the cops. She'd spent her career as a civil rights attorney, only dabbling in criminal defense when it involved protesters being arrested or high-profile police brutality cases. She hadn't been appointed by the governor—she was too politically toxic for that. She gained the bench the old fashioned way: she ran for it. And won handily. No one had run against her since. She didn't owe her position to anyone, and she wasn't going to rule a certain way just to make somebody happy.

So Brunelle prepared himself to be unhappy.

Edwards, on the other hand, seemed almost giddy as they walked into Grissom's courtroom.

"Do you want to just give me that name now?" she teased. "It would save a lot of time."

Brunelle forced a smile. "Does your client want to plead guilty now? That would save even more time."

Edwards offered a polite laugh. "You know I can't do that, Dave. This will be a trial. Everyone is just going to have to suffer through it."

Brunelle thought for a moment, Edwards' words tickling an idea in the back of his mind.

There was an old lawyers' saying: *a good lawyer knows the law, a great lawyer knows the judge*. It sounded like some sort of endorsement of nepotism, but what it really meant was that a lawyer should know what makes a judge tick, how to present an argument in a way that appealed to the judge's pre-existing sensibilities. A lawyer won't convince a judge to change her convictions; he needed to convince the judge that his position was in line with those convictions.

"All rise!" announced the bailiff, and Judge Grissom took the bench. The courtroom was empty save the litigants: Brunelle, Edwards, and Kenny Brown. There was no one in the gallery for a preliminary motion to compel discovery.

"Are the parties ready," Grissom asked as she tipped up the court file to read the case name, "on the matter of the State of Washington versus Kenneth Brown?"

Brunelle stood. It was usually important to show proper respect to a judge; with Grissom, it was vital. "The State is ready, Your Honor."

Even calling his side 'the State' added to his sense of impending loss. He wished he could say, 'the People' like the D.A.s in California, but no such luck. He represented the State, the Government, the Man.

"The defense is ready," Edwards said, also standing. At least, Brunelle, thought, she didn't say, 'the accused.' He hated that term. It was hard to hear it without wanting to insert the word 'unjustly' in there somewhere. Which was the point. He imagined Edwards would be using that in front of the jury, and more than once.

"This is your motion, Ms. Edwards," the judge said. "I'll hear first from you."

Edwards remained standing as Brunelle sat down to listen to his worthy opponent. He had a notepad ready, but he knew what she was going to say. He'd read her brief. And all the cases that said she was right.

"Thank you, Your Honor," Edwards began. "As you know, my client is charged with murder in the first degree. He is accused of killing a woman named Amy Corrigan, whom the State alleges was a prostitute in the employ of Mr. Brown. There is no actual evidence that Ms. Corrigan is even dead, let alone that she was murdered by my client. No body has ever been found, and there are no witnesses who claim to have seen Mr. Brown kill or otherwise grievously harm Ms. Corrigan. Instead, the State's theory is that Mr. Brown was the last person to be seen with Ms. Corrigan and, therefore, somehow, he must be the killer."

Brunelle wished that weren't an accurate description of his case, but with the exception of the evidence about Amy not visiting her daughter as one might expect, that was pretty much all he had. All the more reason to protect Linda.

"The State does have a witness, apparently, who saw Ms. Corrigan with my client shortly before her disappearance. I say 'apparently' because they refuse to identify this witness. I have been provided a police report and an interview transcript of this witness, but the State blacked out her name. As a result, I have no way of contacting her to ask her questions about what she stated in her police interview. As the Court can imagine, I might have some different questions than the police."

Grissom nodded at that. Of course. Brunelle looked back down at his legal pad. He hadn't taken a single note yet. He set his pen down. No reason for appearances; there was no jury in the room.

"I have asked Mr. Brunelle for the name and contact information of this witness, but to no avail." Edwards offered a glance at her opponent. "I have worked with Mr. Brunelle for a long time now and have generally found him to be a reasonable prosecutor to deal with."

Well, thank you, Brunelle thought.

"However," Edwards went on, to Brunelle's chagrin, "in this circumstance, Mr. Brunelle seems to be blinded to his ethical duties by his desperation to obtain a conviction in a case where he simply doesn't have enough evidence to convict. Rather than lay his cards on the table and win the case on the strength of the evidence, he is attempting to gain an unfair advantage by preventing me from being fully prepared for trial and hoping that I might, therefore, do a less than effective job in front of the jury."

Brunelle frowned. That wasn't what he was trying to do, or why. He was trying to protect someone from Edwards' murderous client.

"Your Honor," Edwards began summing up, "this is a simple motion with only one just result. The court should order the state to divulge the identity of the witness immediately so that I can be properly prepared to defend Mr. Brown against this most serious of charges. Thank you."

Grissom nodded to Edwards then looked over to Brunelle. He, too, nodded at his opponent's argument, then stood up. He straightened his suitcoat and buttoned it. Then he placed a hand dramatically on counsel table and looked up to the judge.

"Your Honor, may it please the Court," he began, using that outdated phrase all the new attorneys thought they were supposed to say and all the old attorneys stopped saying years ago. "Allow me to begin by acknowledging the conundrum placed before both Ms. Edwards and yourself: how to protect the rights of a criminal defendant while also protecting the public. And let me be perfectly clear: I don't mean protecting the public from Mr. Brown. No, that would be too simplistic. Rather I mean an evil which Your Honor has spent a career fighting: protecting the public from the overreach of government authority."

Grissom raised an eyebrow at that. *Good,* Brunelle thought. I have her attention. A glance to his right showed he had Edwards' attention as well—and maybe a bit of concern.

"The entire criminal justice system is something of a contradiction. The entire system is weighted strongly in favor of the defendant." He raised his hand slightly. "Now, I'm not complaining, mind you. I'm just making an objective observation. To start with, a defendant is presumed innocent. Is that a good thing? Undoubtedly. But it's not as if that were some kind of requirement of a functional criminal justice system. In fact, most countries don't follow that model. In most countries, including very enlightened and socially liberal democracies in Europe, a defendant is presumed guilty. After all, why would someone be charged with a crime if there weren't facts to support the accusation? In fact, I think the reason we keep reminding juries that a defendant is presumed innocent is because that's just not a natural way of doing things. You hear the cookie jar break and come into the kitchen to find your child standing there with chocolate on her mouth, you're not going to presume she's innocent. You know she did it; you just want confirmation. So right from the beginning, the scales of justice are tipped in favor of the defendant. He's innocent, and he stays innocent until and unless the government can prove otherwise."

He paused to assess the faces of his audience, namely Judge Grissom and, to a lesser extent, Edwards. Their expressions were about what he'd expected. They had no idea where he was going with all this. But they also seemed intrigued by that mystery, so he had them hooked. Time to press on.

"Which brings me to another way in which the system is stacked in favor of the defendant. Not only must the prosecution prove the crime, but we have to do so beyond a reasonable doubt. So you can have a situation where everyone in the room agrees the defendant probably committed the crime—perhaps some horrible crime—but the jury is nevertheless ordered to find the defendant not guilty, because the prosecution wasn't able to foreclose every reasonable alternative explanation.

"In addition, a defendant doesn't have to testify, which is all well and good. But the natural thing to do when someone refuses to deny an accusation is to conclude that they probably did it, and that's exactly what is not allowed to happen. I can't argue that a defendant's silence means they probably did it, and the jury is specifically instructed that they cannot use a failure to testify against the defendant in any way. Again, that's exactly opposite of what we do in our normal lives, and that's exactly why we tell the jury over and over not to do it, because they would otherwise."

Grissom finally interrupted. She narrowed her eyes under the still raised brows. "Is there a point to all this, Mr. Brunelle? I'm pretty sure we all took criminal procedure in law school."

Brunelle smiled at the joke. Of course he did; she was the judge. You always smile at the judge's jokes. "Yes, Your Honor. And I was just about to get to it."

Grissom nodded and leaned back, signaling he could go on.

"My point is, we have all these protections for the defendant—and rightly so. We bend over backwards to make sure everything is slanted as far in his favor as possible, that every ambiguity is resolved in his favor, and every close call goes to him. We do that so, at the end of the day, if a jury comes back with a guilty verdict, we can feel comfortable that the defendant really is guilty and an innocent man isn't heading off to prison."

Grissom nodded. "Agreed."

Brunelle pointed slightly up at the bench, in what he hoped was a respectfully muted gesture. "Yes, but there's a cost to this. And the cost is that, in our focus on the rights and protections afforded the defendant, we forget that the whole reason we're even affording the defendant any rights, is because he did something horrible in the first place to land himself here. It's all well and good that a criminal defendant gets the right to remain silent, to confront witnesses, to be presumed innocent. But what about the crime victim who doesn't get any of those rights? What about the domestic violence victim who gets beaten because her husband doesn't like what she served for dinner? What about the convenience store clerk who gets shot because he didn't open the cash register fast enough? What about the prostitute who gets murdered because her pimp is fed up with her skimming off her earnings?"

Edwards stood up. "Objection, Your Honor."

Brunelle looked to her and opened his palms. "What objection? This is argument on a motion, not examination of a witness in front of a jury. You'll get a chance for rebuttal."

"I'll rule on the objections, Mr. Brunelle," Judge Grissom interjected. Then she turned to Edwards. "This is argument on a motion, Ms. Edwards. I understand your frustration at Mr.

Brunelle's insinuation about your client, but you'll get a chance to address that in your rebuttal argument, if you so choose." Back to Brunelle. "You may continue, counsel, although I'd like you to get to that point you promised you were about to make."

Brunelle nodded to the judge. "Yes, Your Honor. Thank you." It was time to wrap it up. "Every criminal defendant should have the rights and protections afforded him, but we shouldn't lose sight of the fact that he is a criminal defendant. He committed a crime. He gets all those rights because he did something so bad that we, as a society, have decided he should be punished for it. We mustn't forget, in our eagerness to protect the rights of the defendant, that the entire point of the criminal justice system is to vindicate the rights of the victimized and hold offenders accountable."

Brunelle paused, long enough to suggest he might be finished. The judge leaned forward and asked, "I appreciate your advocacy, and I'll tell you that I think some of what you said makes sense and some of what you said is debatable, but I don't understand how any of that is relevant to Ms. Edwards' motion to compel discovery of the name of your witness."

Brunelle inclined his head to the judge. "Of course, Your Honor. Here's my point: the only reason any of us is here dealing with this issue is because Mr. Brown is charged with a crime. The court then steps in and safeguards Mr. Brown's trial rights. In so doing, the court is acting as an official government actor. Meanwhile, out there in the community, there is a person who, through no fault of her own, has information which supports the allegation that Mr. Brown committed murder. She provided that information to law enforcement and that information—all of it—has been provided to Mr. Brown so that he might defend himself against the accusations. The entire transcript was provided to Ms.

Edwards and, of course, her client is fully aware of what he did regardless of whether he can be compelled to say what it is.

"The only thing this court can do, and would be doing if it granted Ms. Edwards's motion, is use the power of government to terrorize a private citizen by requiring the disclosure of that private citizen's identity and whereabouts to a man who, first of all, is accused of murdering one of her friends for doing exactly what she did, and secondly, has posted a ridiculously low bail and is out on the streets where he can follow through with exactly the kind of action she fears and which he already has done to land himself in this situation in the first place."

Brunelle brought his hands together in front of his chest. "So, Your Honor, I'm asking you to protect the rights of an innocent private citizen and not use governmental authority to expose her to personal injury or worse. Thank you."

Brunelle sat down, his heart beating a bit fast but maintaining an exterior of calm. A glance at Judge Grissom's face only confirmed that her expression was inscrutable. She pursed her lips and looked over to Edwards.

"Any response?"

Edwards stood up sharply. "Absolutely, Your Honor."

She started in, but Brunelle allowed his mind to wander a bit as it recovered from his tortured, but eloquent, argument. He wasn't going to get another chance to speak and Grissom had likely made her mind up before either of them opened their mouths. Edwards was hitting all the main points: Confrontation Clause, effective assistance of counsel, blah blah blah. There was some indignation, too, at Brunelle's attempts to trivialize a defendant's constitutional rights or somehow equate a victim with a defendant.

Brunelle knew there was no way to equate Kenny Brown and Amy Corrigan. Kenny Brown was still alive.

Grissom was ready to rule as soon as Edwards sat down again. "First, let me say, Mr. Brunelle, that I am both impressed and concerned by your advocacy. Ms. Edwards, you better watch out if he makes those kinds of siren-like appeals to the jury. I appreciate your effort, Mr. Brunelle, to somehow twist yourself into the protector of individual liberty even as you attempt to put this man," she pointed at Brown, "this private citizen, in prison."

Brunelle acknowledged the compliment with a slight nod.

"However, I am not a juror and I am not about to be confused by creative arguments and flowery turns of phrase. I have no desire to endanger or in any other way impact any private member of the community. But that is not what I'm being asked to do. Whether Ms. Edwards chooses to contact this person is her decision, and her action, not the court's. That's not what I'm being asked to do. What I'm being asked to do is protect the Constitutional rights of a criminal defendant. I have no hesitancy to do that."

She pointed a finger directly at Brunelle. "You are to provide Ms. Edwards with an unredacted copy of the witness's statement, as well as the name, date of birth, and current address and telephone. And you are to do that by close of business today."

Brunelle frowned. He wasn't unprepared to lose the motion. He didn't like the judge's timeline, though.

No harm in asking.

"Your Honor, could you possibly give me until the end of the entire day, not just five o'clock? The witness leads a somewhat transient lifestyle. I may need a few hours to confirm her current whereabouts."

Grissom narrowed her eyes as she considered the request. "How about by ten o'clock this evening?" she suggested. "Will that work for you, Ms. Edwards?"

"We have no objection to that," Edwards stood to reply. "It's not like I'm going to rush right out and talk to her tonight."

No, thought Brunelle. *But I am.*

CHAPTER 14

Brunelle had no idea where Linda Prescott was or how to find her. Prosecutors weren't in the business of finding people. That was detective work.

"Montero. Major crimes."

And there were more detectives than just Larry Chen.

"Detective, it's Dave Brunelle again from the prosecutor's office. I need a little help finding one of our witnesses."

"Oh, okay. The Kenny Brown case, right?"

"Sure," Brunelle conceded.

"Who are we looking for?" Montero asked.

"Linda Prescott. She was the last one to see the victim alive. She was one of Brown's girls."

Montero surrendered a dark laugh. "Then she still is one of his girls. They don't get to quit. That's what Amy Corrigan tried to do."

Brunelle frowned. If quitting got you killed, what would snitching get you?

"I need to find her," Brunelle said.

"So do what everybody else does," Montero replied. "Go to

DateNight.com."

"DateNight.com?" Brunelle repeated.

"Yeah," Montero replied. "That's the way most prostitutes work any more. Post an ad, include a cell number, and wait for the texts to start rolling in. Schedule a time and spend the day in your motel room, turning one trick after another. Almost none of the girls just walk the streets any more. The only johns who still drive around looking for a hooker off the streets are creepy old guys who don't know about DateNight."

Brunelle felt his cheeks sear and was grateful again for the non-visual nature of telephone communication. "So, is she just on there as Linda Prescott? Is it that simple?"

"It's almost that simple, but no, she isn't going to use her real name. None of them do. Here, hold on. I'll pull it up right now."

"DateNight?" Brunelle asked. "On your work computer?"

Montero laughed. "It's part of my job, Mr. Brunelle. I don't think anyone is going to think I'm actually looking for a hooker tonight."

"Heh," Brunelle forced a chuckle. "Right."

"Okay," Montero said. "Here she is. Even with all that make up and the weird selfie angle, I recognize her from her booking photo. She's going by 'Anastasia.' Says she enjoys generous men and new experiences."

"Of course she does," Brunelle muttered.

"You need me to do anything else right now?"

Brunelle considered asking Montero to set up a security detail for Linda starting at 10:00, but he knew that was a non-starter. Chen was right; they couldn't do that. The only thing to be done was to warn her, and with all of Brown's other girls watching, a cop wasn't the person to do it.

"No, thanks," Brunelle answered. "I can take it from here. "

CHAPTER 15

Brunelle opted not to look up DateNight.com on his work computer. It would have been part of his job too, but he didn't relish trying to explain to his IT folks why he was using taxpayer resources to troll for prostitutes. Instead, he left work right at 5:00 and hurried home to his laptop where he could peruse the offerings on DateNight.com at his leisure.

Although not too much leisure. He still had to give Linda's name and contact number to Edwards by 10:00. He would have to assume that Brown would have it immediately after that. That gave him just a few hours to warn Linda that her pimp was about to discover she'd snitched him out.

The prevailing joke about snitches was, 'Snitches get stitches.' Brunelle had seen more than one tough-guy-defendant wearing a t-shirt with that phrase to court. Linda would be lucky to get away with just stitches. Brunelle thought of the other phrase he'd heard, cited less frequently, perhaps because of its length, but undoubtedly more apropos in the current situation: 'Snitches are bitches who end up in ditches.'

Ah, the literary glamour of practicing criminal law.

Brunelle didn't want Linda to end up in a ditch. He couldn't protect her round the clock—he didn't have that kind of time, or, honestly, the toughness to out-tough a pimp who beats and murders his prostitutes. But he could warn her, and she could take steps to get the hell out of the area. But not without making arrangements to come back in time for the trial. He still needed her testimony. And he needed her to stay alive long enough to give it.

It was no problem finding her ad on DateNight.com. The problem was bringing himself to text a prostitute. Linda or Anastasia or whatever she was calling herself, she was unlikely to respond to a text that said, 'Hi. Dave Brunelle, prosecutor, here. Do you have a few minutes to discuss a personal safety plan?' Besides, he would have to assume that Kenny the Pimp or his other girls might read whatever text he sent. What he needed to tell her had to be spoken word only. That left one option.

'Hey, Anastasia,' he typed into his phone. 'Saw ur ad. I want to be generous if u want a new experience. Tonight?'

He only paused for a moment before hitting, 'Send.' It was barely a few moments after that before he got a response.

'11:00. pacific motel. room 311. 100 roses for 30 mins. 150 roses for 60. Extra is extra.'

Great. He had a date. $100 for half an hour, $150 for a full hour. *A good deal,* he supposed. And anything too kinky would cost extra.

"Seems fair," he mumbled to himself. Then he texted 'Ok. C u then,' to confirm the date.

He frowned slightly. He would have preferred something before 10:00 p.m., but he didn't suppose it mattered. He could use his remote desktop program to send Linda's name and number to Edwards' work email at 9:59 p.m. Not even Edwards would stay at the office until 10:00 p.m., so she wouldn't open it until the next morning anyway. He hoped.

He was distracted enough by thoughts of email logistics that he forgot for a moment to feel nervous about having just solicited a prostitute—which, of course, was a crime. Only a misdemeanor, but still, prosecutors weren't supposed to go around committing crimes. Particularly not embarrassing sex-related crimes that would land him and his boss on the front page of the paper. And him in jail overnight.

But the trepidation wasn't at bay for long and after confirming his plan to email Edwards a minute before Grissom's deadline, Brunelle realized what he was doing and reeled at the explosion of nervous bile in stomach.

"What am I doing?" he asked aloud.

But then he remembered what he *wasn't* doing. He wasn't really soliciting a prostitute. He was just setting up a meeting with a witness.

"A witness interview," he assured himself.

Then he smiled at himself. If he were prosecuting a john who used that excuse, he wouldn't believe it either.

He looked at his phone display. He had several hours before his 'witness interview.' He considered having a drink or two, but decided not to add a DUI to his solicitation charge. Instead he set two alarms—one for 9:55 to send his email, and the other for 10:30 so he'd have time to get to North Aurora Avenue by 11:00—then turned on the TV and tried to lose himself in the day's sports scores.

* * *

The Pacific Motel was just two motels up from the Aurora Motel. Brunelle hadn't been far off when he'd tried to find Linda on his own. He just didn't realize she wouldn't be on the streets. Instead, she was in room 311.

Brunelle pulled into the parking lot and found a parking

spot in the back. The clock on his dashboard said '10:53.' He considered parking where he could see room 311, but he didn't really want to be seen, and he really didn't want to see the 10:30 appointment leaving. It might be a witness interview, but it was still with a woman who was being victimized by pimp and john alike, and he didn't like being quite so close to the action.

Being a prosecutor was nice, he considered. He could be on the good guy team, fighting injustice, holding the bad guys responsible, and generally championing the greater good. But he could do it from the comfort and distance of his desk. He got to look at the witness statements and scene photos without actually having to meet the witnesses or process the crime scene himself.

There was something different about homicides too. It was the worst crime, the most permanent. There was no returning the stolen goods and writing a letter of apology. No undoing what was done. But there was also no direct interaction with the victim, and, as final as the result was, there was no chance of the victim being re-victimized. Not like the wife being abused by her husband or the child being molested by his uncle.

Or, Brunelle knew, the prostitute being used by john after john and beaten by her pimp.

He looked again at the clock. 10:57.

Was he really going to go into some seedy motel room, to talk with a woman who was turning trick after trick that night, to warn her that her pimp was about to find out that she was the one who snitched him out? He'd beat her just for not making her quota that night. And what if she didn't care? What if she was more afraid of not earning enough money that night than she was about what might happen tomorrow?

"Oh, shit." Brunelle suddenly realized he hadn't brought any money. Not $100 anyway. She was probably going to be more concerned about explaining why she gave some guy a half hour appointment without getting paid than anything about potential witness intimidation.

10:59.

There was probably an ATM around somewhere. Maybe the manager's office? But was he really going to give a hooker $100? Wouldn't that actually be a crime? Well, not if he didn't have sex. But who would believe that?

11:00.

What if she turned on him? What if her loyalty to Brown was greater than any fear she had of him? What if she was smart enough—or Brown was—to realize they could accuse him of coming to the motel to pay her for sex? That wouldn't just ruin his case; it would ruin his career.

11:01.

Brown could be hiding in the bathroom for all he knew—and Brown would recognize him from court. It would be Brunelle's word against theirs. And he'd sent that stupid text.

Why, people would ask, didn't you just have the detective talk to her? 'Because I didn't want to endanger her,' he would say. 'Mm-hmm, a likely story,' they would respond.

11:02.

His heart was racing almost as fast as his thoughts. His palms were sweaty on the steering wheel, which he suddenly realized he was gripping so tightly his knuckles were white.

He let go and tried to calm his mind.

11:03.

Was he really going to get out of his car, and walk across the parking lot, and knock on the door, and go inside, and close the door, and tell this woman—who was probably high right then—that he wasn't going to give her any money, but instead he was a prosecutor, but don't worry, he wasn't going to arrest her or charge her or anything, he just came to warn her out of the goodness of his heart?

Really?

11:04.

No.

He wasn't going to do that.

He wasn't a cop. And he wasn't a hero.

He was a prosecutor. Prosecutors go to court, not prostitutes.

11:05.

He started his car again and quickly pulled out of the parking spot. He drove too fast past room 311 and pretty much cut off two cars as he turned too widely onto Aurora Avenue, then straightened out and floored it.

He didn't care. He needed the drive.

He turned the rearview mirror to look himself in the eye.

"What the hell were you thinking?" he asked.

He didn't even see the police lights behind him, turning into the parking lot of the Pacific Motel.

CHAPTER 16

It was a long, restless night. Even after the glass of scotch he poured between the front door and the bed, Brunelle didn't sleep well. Troubling dreams stayed just out of memory's reach and he couldn't ever seem to get comfortable. When his alarm went off, he was almost relieved to stop trying to sleep.

By the time he got to the office, he'd already drained most of a grande americano. It would be the first of several that day, he knew. Chain-caffeinating.

The message light on his phone was flashing, and he knew there were at least a dozen new emails in his in-box, but the first order of business was calling Montero. If, as was apparent, Brunelle couldn't warn Linda, somebody had to.

But he got her voicemail.

'This is Detective Julia Montero with the Seattle Police Department. I'm away from my desk, so please leave a message and I'll call you back. Thanks.'

He hated leaving voicemails.

"Uh, Detective. It's Dave Brunelle. From the prosecutor's office. I was just calling because, uh, well, can you just call me back?

It's about Linda Prescott. Okay. Great. Uh, bye."

He reminded himself to be grateful he didn't have to deliver closing arguments over voicemail.

There were actually fifteen new emails, half of them from county-wide spam accounts letting him know about the latest retirement in the parks department and the upcoming sewage maintenance subcommittee meeting, open to the public!

His three voicemails were equally uninteresting. The first was from the legal assistant who ran the file room; she was looking for a file he was pretty sure he didn't have. The second was from the property room asking if they could release something to someone on one of his old cases. The third was a hang up.

Brunelle looked around his desk for a suggestion of what to do first that day. The obvious answer was to crack open the Kenny Brown/Amy Corrigan file and start doing some preemptive legal research on Edwards' imminent motion to dismiss for lack of *corpus delicti*.

Brunelle felt the same about legal research as he did about exercise. He knew it was good for him, and he did it occasionally when compelled, but that didn't mean he liked it. He reluctantly opened his browser to the legal research website the county had decided was good enough for the prosecutor's office and stared at the log-in screen.

Maybe I should check in with Nicole, he thought. *I mean, just in case. See if there's anything pressing going on right now.*

He knew it was bullshit, but he also knew he wasn't quite ready for a morning of slogging through appellate decisions on his computer screen. He pushed himself to his feet and walked, slowly, to the desk of his legal assistant.

"Hey, Nicole. Any new homicides last night?"

Nicole shook her head and smiled. "Afraid not, boss. Looks

like it was a quiet night in the Queen City."

Brunelle cocked his head. "I thought Seattle was the Emerald City."

But Nicole shook her head. "Queen City was the original nickname. King County, Queen City. They switched it because some idiot thought Queen City sounded like there were a lot of gay people in Seattle."

Brunelle thought for a moment. "There are a lot of gay people in Seattle."

"I know," Nicole replied.

"That makes no sense."

"'Right. And renaming it after the Wizard of Oz is even stupider."

"What about 'Rain City'?" Brunelle suggested. "I think I've heard that."

"Or Jet City," Nicole offered. "There's a pizza joint on the Eastside called 'Jet City Pizza.'"

"Jet City, huh?" Brunelle tried it on. "Because of Boeing?'"

Nicole shrugged, "I guess so."

Brunelle considered his options for a moment. "Let's go with Rain City. l like that one best."

Nicole nodded. "Agreed. Rain City it is." Then, remembering how the topic had started, "No homicides in Rain City last night, boss."

Brunelle breathed a sigh of relief. "Good."

He turned and made his way back to his office. That was good news from Nicole. There was time still for Montero to warn Linda. But when he returned to his desk, his message light was on again.

"Dave, it's Chen. Linda Prescott is dead."

CHAPTER 17

"Dead?" Brunelle asked as soon as Chen answered his phone. "How? When? What happened?"

"Last night," Chen answered, ignoring Brunelle's lack of greeting. "We're still working on the 'what happened' part."

"But Nicole just told me there were no homicides last night," Brunelle protested.

"It's not a homicide," Chen explained. "Not yet anyway. Looks like an O.D. Anonymous caller directed units to the Pacific Motel last night. Found her unresponsive in her bed, needle still in her arm."

"Shit," Brunelle exhaled. "What time did they find her?"

Chen took a moment to respond. "The 911 log says the call came in at 2259. First units arrived at 2307."

Double shit, Brunelle thought to himself. If he'd gone into that motel room, the cops would have found him with a dead hooker. That would have been difficult to explain.

"She was pronounced dead on arrival at the E.R.," Chen continued. "But cause of death is still undetermined. At least until after the autopsy. That's why I'm calling you."

Brunelle was confused. He'd assumed Chen had called because Montero had forwarded him Brunelle's message. "I thought you said it was an overdose."

"I said, it *looked like* an overdose," Chen corrected. "But it's pretty suspicious. She was our main witness, and now she's dead. I'm about to head down to the M.E. for the autopsy. You should go, too."

"The medical examiner?" Brunelle practically choked on the words. "Uh... I don't know, Larry. I mean..." But he didn't know what he meant.

Chen could hazard a guess. "You mean you don't want to see Kat."

Brunelle wasn't sure what to say. Which said it all.

"Look, Dave," Chen said. "I thought about what you said, and you're right. I don't really know how your relationship with Kat was. You guys seemed good together, and you seemed pretty damn happy for a while there. So I liked that. But whatever, it's your business. But I still have to work with her, and so do you. This is a big deal. We've got one dead hooker on our hands, and now the one witness who could hold the murderer responsible is dead too. That's suspicious. I need to be at that autopsy, and, quite frankly, so do you. So, man up, and do your damn job."

Brunelle was a bit stunned by the soliloquy, but then he smiled. "Okay, Larry. Fair enough. Thanks. I'll—I'll be there."

But as he hung up, the smile faded. Kat was going to be there, too.

CHAPTER 18

'King County Medical Examiner.'

Brunelle frowned at the words on the sign outside the door to the M.E.'s office.

For people who didn't know what a 'medical examiner' was, the words were unremarkable.

For people who knew 'medical examiner' was the new word for 'coroner', the words were creepy.

For Brunelle, the words were terrifying.

Not because of the dead bodies, but because of the live ones standing over them. One live body in particular.

He hadn't seen Kat for a long time. Too long, arguably. But, then again, he didn't mind avoiding the arguments, recriminations, and guilt likely to accompany any such interaction. It was no coincidence that the latest case to consume his focus was the only one in his file cabinet that had no body. And, therefore, no autopsy. No medical examiner.

No Kat.

He shook his head against the thoughts invading his brain and glanced around the lobby. It was one of the least welcoming lobbies he'd ever had occasion to enter. There was no receptionist, no chairs, just a metal squawk-box by the elevator to buzz the staff who were upstairs in the examining area.

Brunelle had hoped Chen might have waited for him in the unlobby, but no such luck. He glanced up at the institutional clock on the wall—the only thing even close to a decoration. Chen said he'd be there by 10:00. It was already 10:15. Chen wasn't one to wait around for someone else to arrive; he was definitely upstairs already. Brunelle was going to have to go into the lion's (or Kat's) den alone.

He sighed, then pressed the button on the intercom. "Hello? This is Dave Brunelle from the prosecutor's office." He recalled all the times he'd followed that with 'I'm here to see Dr. Anderson' then said, "I'm meeting Detective Larry Chen here."

There was a pause, then a staticky male voice replied, "Okay. Come on up."

The secure elevator dinged and the doors slid open. Brunelle stepped inside, pressed '2', and tried not to throw up.

When the doors opened, his unease was distracted slightly by the combination of the familiarity of his surroundings and the mental effort at recalling a place he hadn't been to for a while. The respite was short lived, however.

"David."

It was Kat, her black hair a bit longer than he'd remembered, her curves more alluring—a fist on her hip, almost as if to make sure he noticed what he'd been missing. She wore a white lab coat over her clothes, blue latex gloves on her hands, and an inscrutable expression on her face. She didn't look happy, he could tell that much. The rest she kept hidden.

"Kat," he replied as he stepped off the elevator. His gaze bounced quickly off of his ex and searched the room for Chen. His buffer. He wondered if he could actually get Chen to remain physically between them at all times they were there. Not likely, though. There was no sign of the lawman. "Uh, hey."

Kat scoffed. "Yeah. Hey." Then she turned and headed for the examining rooms. "Larry's in with the body," she called out over her shoulder. "He warned me you'd be coming. Try to keep up."

Brunelle nodded to himself and took a bracing breath. *Well, that could have gone worse.*

Then again, he knew, *there's plenty of time for worse.*

Chen was indeed already in the waiting room. Along with the remains of Linda Prescott. The body had already been transferred from the gurney onto the metal examining table, and Kat was finishing up the external exam. She ignored Brunelle's entrance.

"Extensive bruising to the extremities," she dictated into a handheld recorder, "at various stages of healing. Most appear to be several days to a week old."

"Hey, Larry," Brunelle greeted the detective.

Chen returned the greeting with a silent nod. Kat looked up at Brunelle with a disapproving eyebrow. She was dictating.

"Right," Brunelle responded audibly to the unspoken directive to shut up, which only extracted an even more disapproving eye roll from his ex-girlfriend.

"No other signs of external injury," Kat went on. Then, focusing her attention on the left arm of what used to be Linda Prescott, she addressed the reason they were all there. "Multiple injection sites, again with various stages of healing."

The injection sites were clearly visible, even more so in death, the scabbing almost black against the pale bluish color corpses get when the blood settles to the bottom of the body.

Brunelle noted at least a half-dozen of them and decided he didn't need to count them all to know Linda was an intravenous drug addict. That wasn't really at issue. There was just one issue.

"Is it a homicide?" he interrupted.

Fuck her dictation. She could do that later.

But Kat didn't share his sense of priorities. "Can I finish, Mr. Brunelle?"

He shrugged. "I don't know, Dr. Anderson. How much more to you need to do to determine whether she was murdered?"

"If she had a knife sticking out of her chest, it would be pretty simple," Kat replied coolly. "This is a little more subtle."

"She was the main witness in a murder case against her pimp, and the day her name is released, she's found dead. That doesn't seem very subtle to me."

Brunelle was vaguely aware of the fact that they were arguing about what they weren't really arguing about.

Kat stood up and crossed her arms. That damn hip stick out again, alluring even under the lab coat. "And you're the expert on subtlety, is that it?"

Brunelle pulled himself up. "I can be subtle."

"You can be a jackass," Kat replied with a dismissive exhale. "Subtle isn't making out with a teenager in the courthouse hallway."

Brunelle felt a blush sear his cheeks, but only half out of embarrassment. The other half was anger. "She's not a teenager. And we didn't make out."

"Fine," Kat spat back. She wasn't quite yelling, but her voice was definitely elevated. "Very subtle. Perfectly professional. You're the pinnacle of polite society. How dare I question the great David Fucking Brunelle?"

Chen finally stepped in. "Uh, guys. Can we do this later? I'd like to stick to business, if we can."

"That's what I was trying to do," Brunelle protested, as if to a teacher who'd caught him fighting on the playground. "She started it."

"Really, David?" Kat shook her head. "Maybe you're the teenager."

Brunelle was about to say something back—or at least was trying to think of a comeback, which was irritatingly not leaping into his brain just then—but Chen interceded again.

"Maybe he's a prosecutor. Maybe I'm a cop. And maybe you're a medical examiner." He pointed to Linda. "And maybe she was murdered."

That was enough to suck the air out of the budding ex-lovers' quarrel that threatened to derail the examination.

Kat returned to her professional detachment. "It's extremely difficult to label this a homicide, Larry." But she still made sure to address Chen, not Brunelle. "I can tell you she died from an excess of heroin in her system, but how it got there—I don't know, except to say that it was injected. If she was murdered, it was because somebody injected her with too much of it. And that's beyond my ability to tell from an autopsy."

"But it's possible?" Brunelle ventured. Just because she didn't really want to talk to him didn't mean they didn't have things to discuss.

"Of course it's possible," she replied, a bit sharply. "But that's not what I do. I don't deal in the possibilities. If she did have a knife in her chest, I'd say she died from sharp force trauma. But I don't know what happened before that. That's what you two do. Gather the other evidence to explain why the cause of death—heroin, a knife, whatever—was or wasn't murder."

Brunelle frowned, but didn't say anything. He already knew

what she was telling him. The autopsy was one piece of evidence, but it never told the whole story.

"Is there any evidence she was held down, or already high or something, so that someone could have injected her with an overdose?" That was all he could hope for, and, somehow, he still placed hope in Kat Anderson.

But she was a scientist, not a hope-monger. "Nothing definitive. She has bruising, but she lived a rough life. There are no other injuries to suggest she was bound or anything. Maybe she was passed out. Who knows?" She looked to Chen again. "You said she was found in a motel room. I presume she was working. Maybe you could try to find out when her last trick was. I mean, if she was about to turn another trick, she probably wouldn't be passed out."

Brunelle's heart jumped. The last thing he needed was Chen poking around, trying to find Linda's last scheduled appointment the night she died.

"Uh, well, I guess there's nothing more you can really do," he said to Kat. "Except, I mean, could you maybe just list the manner of death as undetermined?"

Kat's eyes flared. "Undetermined? It's not undetermined. She died of an overdose. I'll need to wait on the full tox report to confirm, but there's no doubt that's what caused her death."

"Right, but whether it's homicide or accident is your call," Brunelle countered. "Can you just wait a bit before you declare it an accident? I mean, if you're not willing to call it homicide right now, can't you do me a favor and at least put undetermined?"

Kat's eyebrows shot up. "Do you a favor?" she repeated. "You want *me* to do *you* a favor?"

Brunelle grimaced. He understood the subtext. "Um... Yes?" he said anyway.

Chen had completely faded away, either by actual step

backward or emotional insignificance—Brunelle wasn't sure and barely noticed. His attention was consumed by the woman across from him.

"I don't believe this was an accident," Brunelle said. "The marks on her arms show she was an addict. The fact that she was at that motel shows she was working that night." That, and his own 11:00 p.m. 'appointment.' "That means she knew how much to give herself safely, and she had reason to stay alive that night."

But Kat shook her head. "That's supposition, David, and argument. The realm of detectives and lawyers. But I'm a doctor. That's not what I do."

Brunelle nodded. "I know. That's why it's a favor."

Kat surrendered the smallest of smiles, willfully forced into the corner of her reluctant mouth. But she shook her head again. "You know I can't, David." Brunelle grinned too, but a pained grin, and cast his eyes downward.

Kat waited a moment, then said, "I'm sorry, David."

Brunelle looked up and for the first time since he'd arrived at the M.E., he looked Kat in her beautiful dark eyes. "I'm sorry too, Kat. I'm truly sorry."

CHAPTER 19

Favors are for friends.

Linda Prescott's death certificate arrived a few days later and it unambiguously listed her manner of death as 'accident.'

Brunelle wasn't surprised, but he allowed himself to be disappointed. Not in Kat. Just in the impact it had on his case. It would be a lot easier to stand up in front of a jury on a double murder case where he had at least one of the bodies. Instead, he was left with the same weak case.

No, that wasn't true. It was weaker. His one witness was gone. What had been a circumstantial case had turned into a suppositional one. He was going to have to figure out how to save it. But he knew whose fault it was. And it wasn't Dr. Kat Anderson's.

"Jessica," Brunelle almost growled when he ran into Edwards in the Pit later that day. "Well done."

Edwards was seated at a long table with several other attorneys. She turned from her negotiations with another prosecutor in Brunelle's office—a newer guy in the special assault unit—and smiled up at her counterpart. "Why, thank you, Dave." She mistook it as a friendly greeting. "I'm sure it was. What did I do so well?"

"You had my star witness killed," Brunelle replied grimly.

The Pit was usually full of the background noise of a half-dozen or more conversations, people talking over each other and generally doing their best to settle cases and catch each other up on how their weekends went. But the kind of comment Brunelle has just unleashed had the ability to cut through the din and grab people's attention. The lawyers closest to Brunelle and Edwards stopped and looked up at Brunelle looming over one of the most talented and most respected defense attorneys in the county. She cocked her head at him. "Excuse me?"

"Linda Prescott," Brunelle said. "She's dead. Only hours after I gave you her name. What did you do, text the name to your guy as soon as I emailed you?"

Edwards' smile melted away, and her jaw set as she stood up to face Brunelle. She was at least a half-foot shorter than him, even in her heels, but her presence was more than equal to his. "I'm entitled to the names of the witnesses against my client, and I'm entitled—no, ethically required—to share that information with my client in order to provide him the best possible defense. Whatever conversations I had with my client after that are none of your goddamn business."

"They're my business if they result in my witnesses getting killed," Brunelle insisted.

Edwards crossed her arms. "Was she murdered?"

Brunelle felt a nervous pang in his stomach at the question. He hadn't failed to notice that half the room was listening intently, with the other half trying to figure out why everyone else had suddenly stopped talking. He wasn't about to admit defeat. "It's still being investigated."

Edwards' smile returned, but this time it was cold and

mocking. "So, no," she translated.

"She's dead," Brunelle repeated. "And now my case may be too."

"Boo-fucking-hoo for you," Edwards scoffed. "I'm not the one who filed murder charges based on the word of a single prostitute."

"Her being a prostitute has nothing to do with it," Brunelle shot back.

But Edwards disagreed. "Of course it does. She's a drug addict and a liar. She gets taken into custody for hooking, so she throws her pimp under the bus to get a deal. Classic impeachment."

"Classic knowledge," Brunelle countered. "Who else is going to know how Brown treats his prostitutes than one of his own girls? You know as well as I do that most of the witnesses to the cases we do are no angels themselves. Pimps and drug addicts hang out with their own. Nothing good happens after two in the morning, and by then all the good people of the world are tucked away safe in their middle-class beds. I can't pick my witnesses."

"No," Edwards agreed, "but I can pick them apart. And if I don't, I'm not doing my job."

"Well, no worries, Jessica. You did your job. My witness is dead." He hesitated, not wanting to admit his next thought. But then he divulged it anyway, even if just for the dramatic effect. "And so is my case."

Trial lawyers were showmen at heart.

Edwards raised an eyebrow. "Oh, yeah?" She smelled blood. Showman's blood.

Brunelle felt a flash of heat at his collar. He'd given away too much. He became acutely aware of the roomful of attorneys watching him—prosecutors and defenders, allies and opponents—and knew his next response had better be measured.

"Well, maybe not completely dead." He tried to step back from the edge of Hyperbole Cliff. "But it's damaged. And…" And what? 'And you killed her!'? He couldn't say that. Not credibly.

Damn it. Not only had he said too much in admitting his case was fatally wounded, the entire conversation was saying too much. He was mad at the conclusion on Linda's death certificate, and he was taking it out on Edwards.

Edwards narrowed her eyes. She was also clearly aware of the crowd, like a winning boxer drawing strength from the cheers. "And what?" she demanded.

Brunelle frowned. Time to dial it down. "And I just wish you hadn't pushed so hard," he said quietly. "I gave you her name, and now she's dead."

Brunelle's suddenly calmer tone seemed, if not to disarm Edwards, to at least confuse her. "So, what? I have blood on my hands, is that it?"

Brunelle shrugged. "Your words, not mine."

So much for dialing it down.

Edwards didn't say anything for several seconds, but Brunelle noticed her hands ball into fists at her sides.

"The only blood," she snarled, "that I'm going to have on my hands is the blood from your case. Because I'm going to kill it. Expect my motion to dismiss for lack of *corpus delicti* by the end of the week. It will demolish you."

Brunelle grimaced inside. He expected it likely would. But the showman was still aware of the audience. He smiled, seemingly confident. "I'll look forward to it."

Edwards returned the smile, her confidence assuredly genuine, but she didn't say anything. Instead, she held his gaze for several challenging seconds. Then she broke off and turned away.

Brunelle exhaled. He allowed his rushing blood to slow. In

his peripheral vision, he noticed the crowd start to dissipate. He decided not to make eye contact with any of them. The show was over. The showman was ready to slip backstage.

Brunelle walked out of the Pit and started heading toward the elevators when a voice called out behind him.

"Dave."

It was Robyn Dunn. She must have been in the Pit.

He stopped in his tracks. He took a deep breath to steel himself. Then he turned to face her.

Damn. She was just as beautiful as ever. Maybe more. Even with the scowl she wore.

"That was too far, Dave."

He didn't step toward her. They were too far apart for comfortable conversation. They were too far apart, period. But neither of them stepped toward the other.

"It was true," he answered.

But Robyn shook her head. "You don't accuse a defense attorney of having blood on her hands for doing her job. And you really don't accuse Jessica Edwards of that."

"If the blood stain fits."

He didn't want to argue with her. He wanted to kiss her.

"You don't mean that," she replied.

He didn't. He was just angry.

"I used to respect you," she said.

That stung. "Used to?"

"I still want to."

Brunelle thought for a moment, taking the time to drink in her resplendence. "You want me to concede defeat? Is that it? Just let the case be dismissed?"

Robyn frowned. "No. That's not worth respecting. I want you to do your job. And do it well. But I also want you to understand that's exactly what Jessica is doing." She paused. "I thought you understood that."

Of course he understood that. That's what was pissing him off. Or maybe not.

Maybe it was Kat, ignoring his request to wait and signing off on 'accident,' and he was taking it out on Edwards.

Maybe it was Edwards, trash-talking him in the Pit, and he was taking it out on Robyn.

Or maybe it was Robyn, leaving him standing there in the courtroom hallway, his cheek still warm from her goodbye kiss, and he was taking it out on everybody.

"Are you done?" he asked.

She hesitated, then smiled, lighting up her eyes and popping that one beautiful dimple onto her face. "For now. But watch yourself, Mr. B. You're a better man than what you just did.

Brunelle didn't have a reply. He wasn't sure she was right. Either way, he was getting tired of people expecting more of him.

"Maybe," he finally said. Then, with a slight shrug, he added, "Thanks."

He turned to walk away, but he expected her to call out after him again.

She didn't.

God, he missed her.

CHAPTER 20

A few nights later found Brunelle sitting at his desk well after hours, the sky dark outside his windows and his face lit by the pale glow of his computer monitor.

He'd said goodnight to the parade of other employees going home for the night. The legal assistants leaving right at 5:00, followed closely by the majority of attorneys ready to call it a day. Then the handful of prosecutors who were currently in trial, staying late to call witnesses and prepare for the next day. Finally, the cleaning staff, wishing him a good night even though he was still sitting at his desk in his full suit. He hadn't even loosened his tie. His attention was directed squarely at his computer screen.

In anticipation of Edwards' motion to dismiss, he decided to go over all the police reports again, everything he had, to get straight in his head how he was going to show the judge—and, eventually, the jury—that Amy Corrigan had in fact been murdered.

That was going to be the thrust of Edwards' brief. How can Kenny Brown be convicted of murder if there's no proof anyone is actually dead? And if he can't be convicted—if, as the legal standard will be, no reasonable jury could find that Brown had murdered someone—then the judge should dismiss the case prior to trial. No one should have to sit through a trial where the jury couldn't possibly find him guilty.

The response, the only response, was that there was enough evidence to allow a jury to infer she was dead. They might not—and that was another problem he'd be facing if he won the motion—but they should be allowed the opportunity. His legal argument would focus on an appeal to the judge that she shouldn't take the case away from the jury. But he was going to need an emotional argument to get over the hump.

That meant humanizing and presenting Amy Corrigan in a way that the judge would not only agree that there was sufficient evidence to allow the jury to consider the case, but she would want them to. For Amy's sake.

Brunelle started where a prosecutor might naturally start: Amy's criminal history. He pulled the paperwork for her prior convictions and ordered the reports for every time she'd been arrested or charged. It was a lot. She'd been arrested more than a dozen times. Mostly misdemeanors: petty theft, possession of drug paraphernalia, prostitution. Lots of prostitution arrests. Only a few were charged. Generally, his office tried to avoid re-victimizing women who were beaten by pimps to have sex with johns. But the cops couldn't always look the other way, and sometimes the best way to get someone to a safe place for the night was to book them into the jail.

It was a sad story. Reading the police report narratives in order revealed a young woman who'd gone from troubled and fiery to drug-addicted and broken. Initial contacts usually ended in some sort of resisting-arrest scenario, either running from the cops, or trying to kick them in the crotch. By the end, they were ending with a heroin needle in her purse and an inability to carry on a coherent conversation.

Poor Amy.

Poor Lydia.

Brunelle split the reports into those before and those after her daughter's birth. There was a cause for hope in those first few after Lydia was born. Amy insisting she was trying to get out of the business, showing the cops that she was clean, no drugs in her purse or her bloodstream. But, eventually, it crashed even harder. The drugs went from marijuana to crack to heroin. The times between arrests became shorter. But even in the last of them, her lifestyle and drug addiction beginning to overcome her completely, she was cognizant of her daughter.

The last report before her disappearance—her *death*, Brunelle reminded himself—actually carried a heart-breaking trace of hope. She'd been picked up for prostitution loitering. The cop who'd made the arrest called for another unit to do the transport to the jail. That second officer's report was understandably short, just a paragraph. After all, the only thing he did was drive her five blocks to the jail. But that just made the quote stand out all the more amid the few short lines the cop bothered to document:

I was dispatched to Occidental Park to transport a suspect to the jail. Upon arrival, I took custody of the subject, CORRIGAN/AMY. I did not ask her any questions during the transport but when we arrived she made the following spontaneous statement: "This is the last time Lydia's mommy is going to get arrested for this." I made no response and escorted her directly to the sallyport for processing.

Brunelle lowered his tired jaw into his hand. Amy had been right, but for the wrong reason. He frowned and pulled up her booking photos. Every booking photo she'd ever had taken was in the computer and could be scrolled through with the simple click of the mouse. It was a time-lapse of a ruined life. The first couple of shots were simple enough: a healthy young woman with a scowl on her face and a chip on her shoulder. But clicking the mouse showed Amy's demise. Her face grew gaunt, her skin leathery, her hair filthy. But the worst was her eyes: angry and defiant at first, but by the end they were dull, unfocused, absent. The result of years of degradation and chemicals.

Brunelle closed out the booking photo window and leaned back in his chair. He could never call a toddler to say her mommy had stopped visiting her. But Amy's parents were still available. And he could maybe get that transport officer to testify about Amy's last official statement to law enforcement. But something was still missing.

Linda Prescott.

Not just missing, but lost forever. Her statements to the cops—the ones he'd heard himself through the two-way mirror—were hearsay. She was dead now, and that might open up more possibilities for their admissibility at trial through some hearsay exception, but this was a criminal case. There was no way around the Confrontation Clause. Brown had the right to have the witnesses against him be real-live humans on the witness stand, subject to cross examination by Edwards—not some detective just repeating what Linda had said, then claiming ignorance when pressed as to how in the world she could possibly know what she claimed.

That was exactly the kind of criminal trials the Confrontation Clause was designed to prevent. No judge would allow Chen to just repeat Prescott's allegations—that would violate poor Kenny Brown's constitutional rights. The bastard.

It was going to be an uphill battle unless Brunelle could

figure out a way to make up for the loss of Linda Prescott.

He clicked his mouse again and re-opened the booking photo window. Amy's most recent photo—the one where she looked half-dead already—was the default image. He looked at it momentarily, his heart sickening at the sight. Then he clicked all the way back to the first one. That was the woman Kenny Brown killed. Slowly. Mercilessly.

He needed to be held responsible.

One way or another.

CHAPTER 21

Edwards' brief did not in fact arrive by the end of the week. It took until the following Monday for her motion to dismiss to hit Brunelle's desk. But whatever pleasure Brunelle had taken from Edwards missing her own self-imposed deadline was more than offset by the fact that she had obviously used the extra two days to make her arguments nearly invulnerable.

The best Brunelle was going to be able to do was create a reasonable suspicion that Amy Corrigan was dead, then ask the judge to let a jury speculate that it was probably her pimp that killed her. A speculation that was undercut by the fact that she could well have been killed by a john—most serial killers preyed on prostitutes because they get in the cars of strange men and aren't immediately missed when they don't return—or died from an O.D. anywhere from Seattle to San Diego to Miami without being identified by local law enforcement. Just some Jane Doe cremated by some coroner who had no idea that there was trial going on in the Great Pacific Northwest.

Brunelle knew it wasn't enough. He also knew Kenny Brown was guilty. Linda Prescott wasn't lying; she just couldn't tell the truth any more.

He was missing something. He knew that too. And he knew he was going to kick himself when he finally figured it out. He just hoped that kick would come before a judge said, 'Case dismissed,' or a jury said, 'Not guilty.'

He picked up Edwards' brief again. A couple dozen pages and filled with case cites and factual summaries he could scarcely contest. And a deftly worded conclusion reminding the court that, despite all sense of justice and decency, the case really wasn't about Amy Corrigan, it was about Kenneth Brown:

In summary, the Court must remain mindful that a criminal defendant enjoys numerous Constitutional rights, obtained through the bravery of our Founding Fathers and defended over the course of our nation's history by equally brave judicial officers against those who might seek convictions, not from evidence, but from expediency and passion. No person should stand trial for a crime the Court knows cannot be proven. This Court has a sacred duty to protect the rights of Mr. Brown and prevent the State, with all its resources, from placing him even once in jeopardy of a criminal conviction and its resultant punishment.

"Amy who?" Brunelle asked sardonically.

* * *

It was another late night for Brunelle, again wishing goodnight to the departing cleaning staff—who didn't even start their work until after 5:00 p.m.

He'd spent the daylight hours distracting himself from Edwards' brief by busying himself with all of the other tasks and duties from his other cases. Detail stuff. Most of it could have been handled by Nicole or another legal assistant. But he wanted to clear his head and give that missing something a chance to reveal itself to his mind. It didn't.

So after Nicole, and Duncan, and everyone else in his office went home for the night, he pulled out Edwards' brief again and started once more from the top.

It wasn't like he had anyone to go home to anyway.

"Damn," he exhaled after finishing page ten—or maybe it was page eleven. Either way, he closed his eyes and rubbed the bridge of his nose. He couldn't decide which was worse: that his case was so weak, or that he was going to have to research and write a responsive brief. Writing briefs was irritating enough, but it was excruciating when he had no law or facts to support his position.

He opened his eyes and looked out his window. He didn't have as good a view as Duncan—he was the boss after all—but his office was high enough up to see the rest of the downtown skyscrapers, their randomly lighted windows bright against the darkened sky. It looked refreshing. And he was definitely burned out.

"Time for a little walk," he told himself, and pushed himself up from the desk. "I just need a little fresh air. Then I can get back at it."

But he left the brief behind and took his keys with him. He knew himself well enough to know that, once refreshed, he would likely decide to go home after all. Even people who live alone need to sleep. Some fresh air might be just what he needed to crash as soon as he got home and not think about the someones who could have shared his bed that night.

CHAPTER 22

The night was cool, but not too bad. *Bracing,* Brunelle told himself. Cold enough to be glad he'd pulled on his overcoat, but not so much to make the walk uncomfortable. If anything, it encouraged a brisk pace. And that, in turn, might encourage brisk thoughts.

Seattle was a lively town. Not one of those Rust-Belt gothams where the downtown emptied out at 5:01 when all the suburbanite office workers fled to the safety of their gated communities miles away from the city denizens they spent the day ignoring and avoiding. The King County Courthouse was on the edge of the older part of downtown, a few blocks up a steep hill from Pioneer Square, once the jumping off point for Klondike gold rushers, and now a jumping off point for well-heeled bar-hoppers.

Brunelle avoided the area, though, because he wasn't looking to drink or socialize. He was looking to think. Cool air and dark skies helped that. So did solitude. The kind of solitude that's on the edge of other people's activity. Hearing others wasting their time had the power to motivate. He glanced down James Street toward Pioneer Square, then turned south and headed toward

Yesler Street and the no man's land between Occidental Park and the International District.

There were still some people about, but they weren't people likely to bother him. They had their own troubles. Substance abuse and criminal warrants were chief among them. And finding shelter for the night. Luckily, it wasn't raining, but park benches get cold overnight.

The anonymity allowed him to descend into his thoughts. He lowered his head and watched his feet consume the sidewalk, almost hypnotizing him with their cadence.

He knew he was missing something. He'd relied too heavily on Linda Prescott's expected testimony. So when it disappeared, he felt as if he had nothing left. But he knew that wasn't accurate. Cases were rarely won or lost on a single witness. The only exception in his experience was when a defendant chose to testify against his attorney's advice and ended up hanging himself. That occurred more often than Brunelle would have thought, but he knew not to expect anything like that in Brown's case. Brown wasn't that stupid. And Edwards wasn't either.

So what other evidence was there? Amy hadn't turned up in the weeks—now months—since her disappearance. She had a daughter, suggesting she wouldn't have just run off. Her parents thought she was dead. But what else? What else?

Brunelle shook his head. He'd been through it all already, again and again. But he wasn't getting anywhere. No convenient bartender or business partner to jump out and save his case this time. He'd have to figure it out himself.

The night air and mesmerizing sidewalk didn't seem to be doing their job.

"Damn it," he muttered—apparently, a bit too loudly.

"You talking to me?" came a voice from the darkness.

Brunelle looked up to face the owner of the voice—a young man by the sound of it. It took a moment, though, in the darkness, until the man stepped out of the shadow of some trees, his location hidden from the streetlights which Brunelle suddenly felt were far too infrequent in whatever part of the no man's land he'd walked to.

The speaker was indeed a young man. A large young man. And homeless by the looks of him. Young plus homeless often meant mentally ill. His appearance bore that out. He was taller than Brunelle by two or three inches, and probably outweighed him as well, despite a life on the streets, although that might have been the layers of shirts and jackets he wore. He had a matted black beard and black hair sticking out under a ski cap. Brunelle couldn't tell if his face was dirty or just gaunt and baggie-eyed. But above the under-eye smudges were bright, excited, potentially deranged eyes. Brunelle braced himself.

"I said," the man raised his voice, "are you talking to me?"

Brunelle glanced around to assess his surroundings. There were a few other figures in the dark but no one else near him. It was several blocks back to the more inhabited area of downtown. He'd only be able to outrun the younger man if the younger man decided he wasn't worth chasing. "No," Brunelle answered. "I was talking to myself."

"Oh!" came the indignant response. "You're too good to talk to me?"

Brunelle grimaced. This wasn't going to go well. "No, no. I just meant, I was lost in thought."

"You didn't even see me, huh?" the man growled. He took a step toward Brunelle. "I'm just invisible to you, is that it?"

Brunelle looked around again. That flight option was growing in appeal. "No, of course not. I'm just—I'm just going for a walk, trying to think through some stuff. I'm sorry if I disturbed you."

Brunelle hoped that might be the end of it. Apologies had a way of being disarming.

But no such luck.

"Disturbed?" Another two steps toward Brunelle. He was within lunging distance now. "You think I'm disturbed?"

Brunelle instinctively took a step back. "That's not what I said." A non-answer, but better than the honest one. One more step toward him and Brunelle was going to make a run for it.

But the man stopped his advance. In fact, his expression suddenly changed, and he took a half-step back himself, looking Brunelle up and down with an exaggerated head bob. "What the hell are you supposed to be? You a lawyer or something?"

Brunelle looked down at his own clothes. Dark suit, dark overcoat, white shirt, red tie. Yep, he looked like a lawyer all right. The only people left in Seattle who wore suits were the lawyers. The techies never wore suits. Even the bankers were in khakis and denim shirts any more.

"Uh," Brunelle started. It was actually a more complicated question than it seemed. He was indeed a lawyer, but he was a prosecutor. You had to be a lawyer to be a prosecutor, but prosecutors were different; they were more like bureaucrats than real lawyers. His usual answer to the question—he got it more often than you'd think, but again no one else wore suits—was something like, 'Sort of. I'm a prosecutor.' But his professional experience told him the large, mentally ill, homeless man might have had a few run-ins with the law. Identifying himself as a prosecutor might be all that was needed to finally set the man off for real. So Brunelle opted for accurate, but uninformative. "Uh, yeah. I'm a lawyer."

The man's expression instantly changed, and, to Brunelle's

surprise, for the better. "Oh yeah?" His expression softened immediately and he took a non-threatening step forward, his palm extended. "Hey, man, you got a card? I got some warrants I need to get cleared up."

Brunelle exhaled. The plight of being a lawyer: no one likes you until they need you. This guy needed a criminal defense attorney, so there was definitely no way Brunelle was going to admit he was a prosecutor. This was his get-out-uncomfortable-confrontation-free card. But speaking of cards, he didn't have any. Private attorneys needed them for exactly this sort of situation, meeting potential new clients. But Brunelle didn't have clients, so he never carried business cards.

"Oh man." He feigned patting his pockets. "I just gave my last one away."

The other man narrowed his eyes. "You don't want me for a client?"

And now it was time for full-blown lying. "Of course I do," Brunelle said, trying to mollify the larger, younger, more excitable man. "I just don't have any cards."

The man's distrusting gaze deepened. "Don't you even want to know what the warrants are for?"

Brunelle shrugged. "Not really. Whatever. I mean, I don't care what they're for. It's just my job to get rid of them for you."

Or it would be, if I were actually a defense attorney. Brunelle glanced around again. If he could extract himself safely, he was walking straight back to the courthouse. Fast.

The man laughed at his explanation. "Yeah, you lawyers are just like hookers. You don't care what you gotta do, so long as you get paid."

Brunelle grimaced at the description. Unfortunately, it wasn't the first time he'd heard lawyers compared to prostitutes.

There were professional similarities.

"Yeah, well. Everybody deserves a defense." He'd heard some true believer defense attorney say that once. It seemed appropriate somehow.

"Even me?"

Brunelle nodded. "Even you."

The man's expression snapped back to the angry one he'd first worn when Brunelle had said 'Damn it' at him. "What the hell is that supposed to mean?"

Aw, shit.

"You think you're so much better than me," the man demanded, "just 'cause you wear a fucking suit?"

That's not the only reason. Brunelle hoped in the dark his expression didn't betray his thoughts. "No, it's just a suit."

The man started nodding. An overly emphatic, not quite lucid nod. "That's right, man. That's right. You just a suit. You just another fucking suit. You ain't no different from the next."

Brunelle just blinked at the no longer scary man.

"You hear me?" the man yelled. "You lawyers are all the same. You're all the fucking same."

"Yeah," Brunelle replied slowly, his own nod just as detached from the real conversation as the homeless man's. "I'm just like a hooker," he said. "And one ain't no different from the next."

CHAPTER 23

The first thing Brunelle did the next morning was call Chen. "Larry, it's Brunelle. We need to talk."

Brunelle expected push-back, maybe some ambivalence. At least an irritated sigh. But Chen was fully on-board, enthusiastic even. "I agree. We do."

That was good, although momentarily disorienting. "Uh, okay. Great. So, here's the thing—"

"No," Chen interrupted. "Not over the phone. We should meet in person."

"Oh, okay," Brunelle replied. He wouldn't mind seeing Chen face-to-face, he supposed. "Should I come down there or you come to my office?"

But Chen demurred. "No. Let's go someplace else. Someplace off-campus. Do you know where the Seneca Street Roastery is?"

Brunelle didn't, but he could guess. "Seneca Street?"

Chen allowed a laugh. "Right. Sixth and Seneca. I'll meet you there in twenty minutes."

"Sounds good," Brunelle agreed. Then, considering lugging

the file and three-ring binders across downtown, "Should I bring anything?"

Chen laughed again, but less mirthfully. "Just your phone."

* * *

Chen had beaten him there, already seated at a tall table in the back corner. Brunelle waved to him, then went to the counter to order a tall americano. After the barista finished his drink, Brunelle pulled out a stool and joined the detective.

"Nice place," Brunelle commented with a glance around the coffee shop. There were only two other people in the place. One was the barista, the other was a scrawny, bearded guy crouched over a laptop a few tables away. "And out of the way. Good idea. What I wanted to talk about might be better discussed here after all."

Chen raised an eyebrow but didn't reply immediately.

Brunelle continued. "I have an idea about what to do about Linda Prescott's death. But I'm going to need your help." He thought for a moment. "Well, maybe not 'need' exactly, but it's probably better if we do this together. I'm not a cop. I have to be reminded of that sometimes."

Brunelle stopped. Chen was listening to him, but he wasn't hearing him. The detective's expression made clear he had something else occupying his thoughts. "What?" Brunelle asked.

Chen frowned and locked eyes with Brunelle. "I found your number on her phone."

Brunelle's heart dropped.

"And," Chen added, "the texts you sent her."

Brunelle felt his cheeks sear, despite knowledge of his own innocence. He raised his palms in protest. "Wow. Okay. No. It's not what you think."

But Chen just shook his head. "What the hell, Dave? First, you throw away your relationship with Kat to fuck someone half your age. Now you're going to hookers?"

Brunelle closed his eyes and exhaled through his nose. "I'm *not* going to hookers. And Robyn isn't half my age. More like two-thirds."

Chen waved the response away. "Whatever. Kat and Robyn are your business. But going to hookers is my business. It's a fucking crime, Dave. Patronizing a prostitute. You want to throw away a great woman, go ahead. But don't throw away your career."

"I wasn't patronizing a prostitute, Larry," Brunelle insisted.

"I read the texts, Dave," Chen countered. "At least you didn't sign your name to them. But Jesus, what were you thinking, using your own phone? I know your number, Dave. It jumped off the screen at me."

"Larry, you're not listening to me," Brunelle interrupted. "I wasn't trying to fuck her. I was trying to warn her."

Chen laughed darkly. "Warn her? For a hundred roses an hour? Must have been one hell of a warning."

Brunelle lowered his head into his hands. "You're not listening to me." He looked up again. "I wanted to warn her that Brown knew she'd snitched him out. I had to hand her name over to Edwards, and I wanted her to know. It was the only way I knew how to contact her."

Chen looked long and hard at Brunelle. "Jesus, Dave, you were her next john. She OD'd right when you were supposed to meet her. Shit, for all I know, you saw the cop cars and freaked out."

"I did freak out," Brunelle admitted. "But I didn't see any cop cars. I just got scared and left."

Chen cocked his head. "Scared of what?"

Brunelle shrugged. "I don't know. Her, Brown, getting caught by those cops who showed up after I left."

Chen leaned forward and lowered his face. "I don't know whether to believe you."

Brunelle looked directly at his friend. "I don't care if you believe me. It's true."

Chen kept his face lowered, but his eyes raised to meet Brunelle's. He chewed his cheeks for several moments. Finally, he shoved himself up again. "Okay. I believe you. You're stupid, but you're not an idiot." Then Chen leaned forward again, resting a forearm on the table. "But I know you, Dave. I know you're not really stupid enough to go to a prostitute. You're just stupid enough to use your own phone to text her."

Brunelle had to laugh. "Fuck you, too, Larry. But, yeah, I guess so."

Chen leaned back in his chair again. "Kat really did you a favor."

Brunelle had been about to reach for his drink, but the sound of Kat's name stunned him. "A—A favor? How?"

"By declaring Linda's death an accident," Chen explained. "If she'd said it was a homicide, I'd have to write a report about finding your cell number on her phone."

"I'd deny it," Brunelle said.

"You just admitted it," Chen pointed out.

"You didn't Mirandize me."

"You're not in custody."

"Damn." Brunelle took a sip of his coffee. "You win."

"No, it's a win-win," Chen replied. "I know you did it, but I don't have to tell anyone."

"Well, good," Brunelle replied over another sip of coffee.

"Yeah," Chen took a casual sip of his own coffee. "You should send her a thank you note or something."

"And you," Brunelle replied, "should shut the hell up."

"Fine," Chen agreed. "But you take my advice, too: stop texting hookers."

"Deal," Brunelle answered. Then, in all seriousness, he added, "I'll go in person."

Chen's eyebrows shot up, but before he could say anything, Brunelle pointed a finger at him. "And you're coming with me."

CHAPTER 24

"Remind me again why I'm here," Chen asked as they pulled into the parking lot of the Aurora Motel.

"Because we both know I shouldn't be out here alone," Brunelle answered as he pulled his car into a parking stall near the manager's office. "Only a detective should do the witness interview."

"And why are you here?" Chen followed up.

"Because," Brunelle put the car in park and turned off the engine, "once the interview is over, only a prosecutor can give her immunity."

Chen grinned, then nodded. He looked around. "So now what?"

"Now we wait," Brunelle answered. "But I don't think we'll have to wait very long."

Sure enough, even as Brunelle finished his sentence, a woman sidled up to their car. "Hey, there. You boys looking for a date?"

It was the same woman as his first trip there. Brunelle recognized her. She clearly didn't recognize him. She saw a lot of men, he supposed, and she probably tried to not remember any of them.

She was probably 20. Brunelle had never been great at guessing women's ages. Her excess makeup and years of life on the street made it even more difficult, aging her beyond her years. She was short, probably 5'3", and a little on the plump side, with large breasts and a bit of a belly. Not that Brunelle was looking. It was just impossible to miss, given the tiny tank top and miniskirt she'd squeezed herself into.

She peered into the car. "Oh, there's two of you, huh? Yeah, I don't do that. But I can get another girl." She looked over to Chen, as if her pairing with Brunelle were settled. "What kind of girl are you looking for?"

"The kind," Chen leaned forward to answer, "who knew Amy Corrigan."

If the woman had been high or drunk—a definite possibility—she suddenly sobered up.

"Amy?" she repeated, an edge of fear all too obvious in her voice. "Why do you want to know about Amy?"

Chen didn't answer. Instead, he nodded toward the back seat of the car. "Get in."

The woman looked at the back seat, but hesitated.

"We can't talk out here in the open," Chen explained.

When she hesitated still, Brunelle added. "We'll pay you for your time."

Brunelle wasn't sure Chen could offer that, but he was willing to. He understood what she really feared.

"He won't beat you," Brunelle assured her. "Not tonight."

A wave of emotions washed down the woman's face, but not all of them were easily identifiable. But Brunelle could read the two that mattered: fear, and hope.

"What's your name?" Brunelle asked her.

There was only the slightest hesitation this time. "Tina."

Brunelle smiled as kindly as he knew how. "Get in the car, Tina."

She nodded. "Okay," she practically whispered. A few moments later, Tina was in the back seat, and Brunelle was pulling out onto Aurora Avenue.

A rolling car was hardly the optimal interrogation room. In short order, they had reached Green Lake, a small inland lake in Seattle's north end. Rather than hookers and drug addicts, the paved path around Green Lake was populated by joggers and baby strollers, even at that late hour. Brunelle turned off Aurora and found a parking spot near the recreation building at the east end of the lake.

They stepped out of the car and found seats at a nearby picnic table. They were hiding in plain sight. Or at least talking in plain sight where no one cared what they were doing. Which was just as good.

Interrogations usually started with warm up questions. Name, rank, and serial number. Simple questions, designed to get background information and test the subject's truthfulness. If they'd lie about their own name, how could you believe whatever they said about the crime?

But this wasn't a usual interrogation. Brunelle sat silently while Chen folded his hands across the table from Tina. "Tell me about Amy," the detective asked.

"Amy? Amy was great." Tina shook her head slightly and looked away, at nothing in particular. "She was sweet, kind, funny. She wasn't the smartest, but if you needed something, anything, she was there for you. She'd give you the shirt off her back." Then she laughed. "I mean, if she was wearing one."

Brunelle smiled slightly at the joke; Chen, too, but less so. It was one thing to be polite, but this was serious business.

"Do you work for Kenny Brown, too?" Chen asked.

Tina's eyes widened just a bit. "No, thank God. I've seen what he does to his girls."

"Are you independent then?" Chen followed up.

Brunelle wanted to jump in, too, but he managed to bite his lip and let the cop do the interrogation. That was the plan. He knew to stick to it.

Tina laughed, but joylessly. "No. You don't get to be independent. Not for long. Too many pimps around. A girl can't keep her money when there's five guys ready to beat her head in for it."

Brunelle frowned. They just used women like Tina. But then again, he realized, what was he doing?

"Did Kenny beat Amy?" Chen continued.

Tina laughed more heartily this time, but she was laughing at Chen. "Well, yeah. Of course." She rolled her eyes. "Like I said, she wasn't the smartest. And Kenny is one mean mother fucker. She kept pissing him off. The girl just never learned."

Brunelle felt his face fall. But Chen kept his poker face. "When was the last time you saw her?"

Tina frowned in thought for a moment. "I dunno. Probably a week before Kenny killed her."

Chen's expression cracked just enough to raise an eyebrow at Brunelle. He turned back to Tina. "How do you know Kenny killed her? Did she say something?"

"No. But he did."

More raised eyebrows, but Chen made no effort to conceal them. "Kenny said he killed her?"

Tina shrugged. "Well, not exactly. He wasn't all like, 'I killed

Amy.' But after she disappeared, he would say shit like, 'You know what I did to Amy? I can do that to you, too.' His girls were scared shitless. And I don't blame them. He's crazy. Everybody knows he killed her. He wanted everybody to know."

Chen leaned back and considered the information. Brunelle considered the rules of evidence and broke his silence. The information wasn't any good if it got excluded as hearsay.

"Did you actually hear Kenny say that stuff yourself? Or did you just hear it from other girls?"

"Both," Tina answered. "All the girls were talking about it. But I also heard him say it a bunch of times to girls I was next to. He wasn't shy about it. Like I said, he wanted people to know about it. He liked people being scared of him."

Brunelle nodded and leaned back. Most of that would be admissible—at least the times she actually heard it herself. Brunelle would need to nail down the exact number of times she'd heard it, and follow up with the prostitutes he said it to, but there would be time for that. The trip had just proved worth it. He could let Chen wrap it up.

"How many times did you hear him say that to someone?" Chen followed up.

Tina shrugged. "I dunno. A few, I guess."

"More than three?"

Tina nodded. "Oh, yeah. Definitely."

"More than ten?"

A frown. "No, probably not that many."

"And which girls?" Chen asked. More prostitutes meant more witnesses. Brunelle and Chen both knew that. Unfortunately, Tina could figure it out, too.

"I don't think I should say," she answered. She suddenly seemed very aware of where she was, and who she was talking to—

as if awakening from a dream. "Actually, I probably shouldn't be saying anything at all." She looked around a bit frantically. "Shit. What time is it?"

Brunelle looked at his watch. "Ten twenty-three."

"Shit," Tina repeated. She jumped to her feet. "I gotta get back. I've been gone for too long."

Brunelle and Chen looked to each other. Brunelle nodded. He had what he needed. A confession by Brown. 'Anything you say can and will be used against you.' Even if it's said to a drug-addicted, street-level prostitute. The only trick would be getting the drug-addicted prostitute to the witness stand.

"Don't worry, Tina." Brunelle stood up too. He pulled out his wallet. "I told you we'd pay for your time."

"No, it's not that. I just..." She started pacing in a tight, awkward circle. "I shouldn't be talking to cops. I'm not a snitch."

"Of course not," Brunelle responded. "You're a friend. Amy's friend."

That was a bit of a gamble. He didn't know whether Tina considered Amy a friend, but he supposed there was likely some camaraderie borne of their shared circumstances. It seemed to penetrate, even if only slightly. Tina stopped her crazy circle and looked at Brunelle, her eyes welling. "No. I'm a whore. A stupid whore. And I just admitted it to a couple of cops."

"I'm not a cop," Brunelle corrected. "I'm a prosecutor."

Tina sniffled. "Oh, big fucking difference."

"There is a difference," Brunelle offered. "I can give you immunity."

Tina's eyebrows raised. Brunelle wasn't sure if from curiosity of the offer, or ignorance of its meaning.

"Full immunity," he went on. "For the prostitution, the drugs, everything. You could start over."

Tina's wet eyes narrowed slightly. She rubbed the back of her hand across her nose. "You can do that?"

Brunelle nodded. "Yes."

But Tina had lived a hard enough life to know there's always a catch. "And what do I have to do?"

Brunelle frowned slightly. "You have to testify."

Tina's eyes flared, sending a tear streaming down one cheek. "Against Kenny Brown? No! No fucking way. You're crazy. I'm not snitching out Kenny Brown."

"You just did," Chen pointed out.

Tina resumed the frantic circle. "Oh, man. Oh, man. No. No, you said we were just talking. You didn't say nothing about testifying. No. Uh-uhn. No way. No fucking way."

They were losing her. The last thing they needed was her panicking and telling her pimp about their meeting, or taking off out of state where they'd never find her. Brunelle needed her calm and nearby. At least until the trial.

"Tina, Tina, relax." Brunelle pulled out a bunch of twenties from his wallet—way too many—and stuffed them into her hand. "That's way down the road. I'm hoping there won't even be a trial. Most cases settle. We could get him dead to rights already on the pimping charges. When I explain to his lawyer that I have a bunch more witnesses about Amy, he'll probably just take a plea bargain and you'll never have to testify."

Tina stopped her pacing again and looked at Brunelle. She didn't say anything, but she was listening.

"If he takes a deal, there's no trial," Brunelle explained. "And if there's no trial, there's no need for witnesses. You'll never have to set foot in a courtroom."

Tina narrowed her eyes again and crossed her arms. "I'm not testifying."

Her need to assert that confirmed for Brunelle that she would do it if compelled. She was trying to stare him down now because she knew she wouldn't really refuse later. But no reason to call her on it just then.

"Understood," Brunelle replied, knowing full well he was going to subpoena her—but not right then. Right then, they needed to get her back to the motel with her hand full of cash, not a subpoena. He nodded toward the money still visible in her hand. "Let's get you back. Thanks for your time."

Tina looked down at the money for several seconds. Then she crumpled the bills and shoved them into her purse. "Thanks for the break," she said. "I hope I never see you two fuckers ever again."

Then she turned and strutted back to Brunelle's car.

CHAPTER 25

The meeting with Tina had been a success. Chen did some follow up and discovered her real name was Jillian Hammond. Maybe 'Tina' sounded sexier—Brunelle didn't particularly think so—or maybe she just didn't want people to know her real name and what she was really doing. Chen's next assignment would be to get the names of at least two other women, maybe three, who had heard Brown make similar statements.

Confessions, Brunelle reminded himself. Edwards would call them just statements, but 'confessions' sounded so much better. Label a statement a confession and the jury won't even care what was actually said. Confession equals guilt.

So Chen's task was to locate those women and lock down their stories. Brunelle's was to draft the response to Edwards' motion to dismiss. He still didn't have a body—a *corpus*—but he had the admission to the bad act—the *delicti*. That would probably be enough. It had to be.

Edwards was a better brief writer than he was. His strength lay in the courtroom, arguing to judges and explaining to juries. He knew he couldn't out-write Edwards, so he just tried to prepare a competent brief and hoped his oral advocacy would carry the day.

He shook his head slightly as he sent his completed brief to the printer. Edwards was a pretty damn good speaker, too.

* * *

The motion hearing wasn't before Judge Grissom. Good news for Brunelle. He wasn't sure he could rely on Judge Grissom to rule for him out a second time. The bad news was that the new judge was Andrew Carlisle. Judges are like any other population: varied. Get 100 construction workers, or software programmers, or ballerinas together, and there will be some who are funnier, kinder, smarter, etc. Judges were no different. And if you assembled the nearly 100 superior court, district court, and municipal court judges in King County, Judge Carlisle would stand out as absolutely, assuredly, without question, the dumbest one in the lot.

He'd been appointed by the governor when a spot opened after an unexpected retirement. He came from a big corporate firm that had donated a lot of money to the governor's last campaign. At first, it just seemed like he just needed a little time, after a career practicing civil law, to figure out the world of criminal law. But it didn't take too long to realize he was never going to get it and that he'd likely been suggested to the governor by the partners of the law firm just so they could be rid of him.

Of course, Brunelle couldn't say any of that out loud. Not on the record, anyway. It was an ethical violation—and, therefore, potential bar complaint—to disparage the bench. But he'd participated in the hallway conversations, and he accepted it all internally, because regardless of intellectual acumen, Carlisle was the judge. Brunelle had to prepare himself not just to argue his point, but to educate the judge in a way that was both effective and subtle so the judge wouldn't think everyone in the courtroom knew he hadn't the first idea about *corpus delicti* law. Even stupid judges hate to be embarrassed. *Especially* stupid judges.

Brunelle walked into Carlisle's courtroom exactly six minutes before 9 o'clock. Enough time to set up his file and notebook and notepad and reference books, but not enough time to sit around wondering if he'd made all the necessary points in his brief, or worse yet, taking out a copy of the brief and rereading it, which would ensure he spotted some egregious typo just as the judge took the bench. It also limited the amount of time for pre-bout small talk with his opponent.

"Good morning, Dave," Edwards greeted him as he placed his things on the prosecution table. Brown was already seated, glancing around absently and looking far too relaxed for Brunelle's liking. The guy ought to be sweating it, at least a little. He was facing a murder charge, for Christ's sake. But Brunelle supposed anyone who could punch a woman in the face to make her have sex with strangers and then take her money probably wasn't fazed by a bright, airy courtroom filled with people in suits. Brown actually looked a little bored. And why not? There was no way Edwards was going to put him on the stand; the hearing was about what Brunelle could—or couldn't—prove, not about what the defense might claim. Brown's presence was required, but not his participation. So everyone had already forgotten about Amy Corrigan, and for the next few hours, everyone could ignore Kenny Brown, too.

"Good morning, Jessica," Brunelle replied. It was a genuinely warm response. Just because they were about to join battle didn't mean they couldn't be friends until then. He straightened his materials on the table, centering his notepad in front of his chair. "This should be interesting with Carlisle."

Edwards raised a knowing eyebrow. "Yes, indeed. I can't

decide who this helps more, me or you."

"Probably you," Brunelle opined with a thoughtful frown. "'No body equals no case' is pretty simple."

"So is 'We wouldn't charge him if he weren't guilty,'" Edwards countered, a bit irritably. "You don't even realize how easy you prosecutors have it. Everybody thinks you're the heroes and we're the bad guys. Hell, all you have to do is show up, look pretty, and the judges and juries fall all over themselves to give you whatever you ask for."

Brunelle thought for a moment. He cocked his head. "You think I'm pretty?"

Edwards' eyes flared at the joke but before she could reply, Judge Carlisle took the bench.

"All rise!" the bailiff bellowed. The attorneys obliged, of course, and a moment later Carlisle took his seat above them all.

"Please be seated," he said as he straightened his robes. The gallery was empty. It was only a preliminary motion, after all, not a trial; but it was a motion to dismiss on a murder case. Normally, that would have attracted at least some of the junior prosecutors or public defenders, but the motion was strictly legal argument, no testimony, and the argument was on an obscure legal doctrine. The crowd would show up for the trial, but, for right then, Brunelle and Edwards had the courtroom to themselves.

Carlisle looked down at the attorneys. Intellectual ability aside, he looked the part of judge: late 50s, thick head of silver hair, wire-rimmed glasses, and wrinkles starting in all the right, wise-looking places. "Are the parties ready on the matter of the State of Washington versus Kenneth Brown? This is some sort of motion or other, correct?"

Brunelle nodded, glad he hadn't wasted too much time on his brief that the judge obviously hadn't read—or if he had, he hadn't bothered to remember. Fine with Brunelle; his brief wasn't exactly a masterpiece of legal advocacy. But Edwards' was. So she was visibly irritated. Especially since it was her motion.

"It's a motion to dismiss, Your Honor," she said. "For lack of *corpus delicti*."

Carlisle nodded. "Right," he said, still nodding.

Edwards forced a smile—to suppress the eye roll, Brunelle knew. "We are asking the court to dismiss the charge because the state cannot establish that a crime even occurred."

Carlisle's brow furrowed. He glanced between the lawyers. "What crime?"

"Murder, Your Honor," Brunelle was glad to answer. He lowered his voice a notch to sound more important, and menacing. "Murder in the first degree."

Carlisle looked back to Edwards. "You want me to dismiss a murder case?"

Edwards exhaled audibly through her nose. "Yes, Your Honor. They can't prove anyone was actually murdered. They don't have a body."

The judge's furrows deepened. "What do you mean they don't have a body? They lost it?"

"They never had it," Edwards answered. "They're speculating she's dead because she went missing."

Carlisle looked back at Brunelle. "Is that true?"

Brunelle knew the honest answer was, 'Yes,' maybe followed by a bit of explanation. But he also knew that direct of an answer wouldn't help his cause. So instead he said, "He confessed to the murder, Your Honor. To several different people."

Carlisle's head swiveled back to Edwards. "Is that true?"

"Allegedly," Edwards replied, "although we don't admit any of those alleged statements. But Your Honor, it wouldn't matter if he'd confessed a dozen times, all on videotape. Under Washington law, a confession alone cannot support a conviction absent some evidence corroborating the confession. For example," she threw her hands open in front of her, "a body."

Carlisle frowned and pushed himself back in his tall leather chair, crossing his arms as he did so. He looked like a cross between a petulant child and a lost traveler. After several seconds of contemplation, he leaned forward. "So let me get this straight. You," he pointed at Brunelle, "want to prosecute someone for murder even though you don't have a body."

Brunelle simply nodded, in a way he hoped appeared confident.

"And you," Carlisle turned his gaze and finger to Edwards, "want me to dismiss it even though your client confessed to it."

"Allegedly confessed," Edwards felt compelled to reply. "And yes, Your Honor, that's exactly what we want."

Carlisle leaned back again, his arms uncrossed this time. "Well, to be entirely honest, counsel, I don't really like either of those options."

Brunelle had to nod in agreement. Those were two bad choices. But he knew how to use that to his advantage. Unfortunately, before he could offer Judge Carlisle a way out of his conundrum, Edwards jumped in.

"I know it may seem strange, Your Honor, but there is a long line of case law in Washington regarding confessions and the *prima facie* evidence necessary to establish *corpus delicti.*"

Brunelle smiled. Edwards had used two Latin phrases in the same sentence. She was definitely going to lose Carlisle if she kept that up. The only thing worse would be a string of case cites.

"In the case of State versus Hamrick," Edwards began, "Division Two of the Court of Appeals affirmed Washington's *corpus delicti* rule even in cases of driving under the influence, holding that mere opportunity to commit a crime was insufficient to corroborate an extrinsic confession."

Brunelle watched Carlisle's face intently. The judge frowned at the case cite, then more so at the idea that Edwards was citing DUI law, then raised a confused eyebrow at the phrase 'corroborate an extrinsic confession.'

"In State versus Aten," Edwards continued, "again a Division Two case, the Court of Appeals…."

Edwards went on to explain how these cases supported her argument that, in Washington anyway, the mere fact that someone confesses to a crime isn't necessarily enough to prosecute them for it. The problem for Edwards was that there was a reason Carlisle hadn't read their briefs: he didn't like the law. Not the academic subtleties of case law, and not the intellectual gymnastics involved in reasoning that finding a crashed car with a drunk guy standing next to it who admits he was drunk driving is somehow insufficient to prove said drunk guy was actually guilty of DUI. That was stupid. It was the law, but it was stupid. And Carlisle knew stupid.

"Now, in the case of State versus DuBois, Division One acknowledged the distinction between the evidence necessary to establish *prima facie* the elements of a crime as opposed to—"

"Ms. Edwards," Carlisle interrupted. "I'm familiar with the law."

That wasn't true, Brunelle knew. What he really meant was, 'Don't bother me with the law.'

"But," the judge continued, "I don't want to get bogged down in all those details. Did your client, or did he not, confess to the murder of, uh…" He flailed around at the papers in front of him a bit, then looked to Brunelle.

"Amy Corrigan," Brunelle was glad to supply the victim's

name.

"Yes, Amy, uh, Corrigan," Carlisle repeated. "Did your client admit to murdering Ms. Corrigan?"

Edwards stood stock still for a moment. "That's what the state alleges."

A lawyer's response. And worth exactly that much.

"Okay," the judge acknowledged both the response and the emptiness of it.

"But they have no body," Edwards continued. "So his confession is irrelevant."

Carlisle raised an eyebrow, "How can a confession be irrelevant?"

"When they can't prove the underlying crime without it," Edwards practically scolded. She was right, technically. But it was a lawyer's position. Overly analyzed and difficult to explain, let alone justify.

Carlisle pursed his lips and cast his eyes to the ceiling. "How am I supposed to decide what to do when there's no body but there is a confession?"

Now it was time to offer Carlisle his way out. "I have a suggestion, Your Honor," Brunelle interposed.

Judge Carlisle looked down from the ceiling. "What is it?"

Brunelle manufactured his most sincere, 'regular guy' shrug. "Don't."

Carlisle cocked his head at him. "Don't?"

"Don't decide," Brunelle repeated. Then he added just the slightest assertive edge to his posture and voice. "Let the jury decide. That's their job. Deny this premature motion to dismiss and let the jury decide if we've proven the charge beyond a reasonable doubt. They'll hear there's no body, and they'll hear the defendant confessed. And they'll hear a lot more on top of all that. And then they can decide. Not you. Them."

Judges didn't become judges to make decisions. They became judges to get a state pension and have everyone stand up when they walked in a room. For a few of them it was about justice, but for most of them it was about money and status—just like everyone else in the world. Making decisions was hard, especially big important decisions between throwing out murder cases or violating defendants' Constitutional rights. If such a decision could be avoided while keeping the pension and admiration, all the better.

Edwards started to protest, "But Your Honor, that's the whole point of this motion. A jury shouldn't be allowed to hear it because it would be— "

But Carlisle interrupted. "I have to agree with Mr. Brunelle. An issue as important as this should be decided by a jury."

"An issue as important as this should never get to a jury," Edwards protested. She pointed at Brunelle. "They don't have a body!"

Carlisle nodded, nonplussed by Edwards' raised voice. "Then I imagine the jury might well acquit your client. But I'm going to decline to do so for you in advance. I'm denying the motion to dismiss and confirming the matter for trial."

Carlisle hurried off the bench before Edwards could argue any more. Brunelle smiled and started to collect his things.

"That was total B.S.," Edwards stormed over to say. "That's not the law."

Brunelle shrugged and offered a boyish smile. "I'm not so sure, but it's the ruling. I get my trial after all."

His smile faded as he considered how much work he had to do to get ready for that trial. If Carlisle had thrown out the case, Brunelle could have blamed him, and the appellate courts, and Edwards, and everyone else under the sun. But now if he lost the trial, everyone would blame him.

"You sure do, Dave." Edwards offered her own, predatory smile. "Be careful what you wish for."

CHAPTER 26

Whatever joy there had been in leveraging Carlisle's simplicity against him was reasonably short-lived. Two weeks before trial, the case was assigned back to Judge Grissom. The next day, Edwards filed her motions *in limine*—all the things she wanted suppressed and excluded during the trial. Motions *in limine* were usually pretty predictable and didn't require much argument. Not like the motions to dismiss Brunelle had managed to fend off. Just procedural things, like excluding witnesses from the courtroom during other witnesses' testimony, and mutually agreeable things, like no hearsay without first laying the foundation for a hearsay exception.

Brunelle had been reading Edwards' standard motion *in limine* brief for so many years that he almost didn't bother thumbing through this one to see if she'd made any changes. Usually the only interesting thing was to see if she'd remembered to change all the references to her client to 'Mr. Brown' from whichever defendant she'd last filed the motions for. It was always fun to imagine a defendant reading a pleading filed on his behalf and coming across an instance of someone else's name, just in case the defendant wasn't already dubious of his representation from the oft-called 'public pretender.'

Fortunately, it was this one small joy that enticed Brunelle to flip through the dozen-page document, and discover the motion buried second-to-last. Putting it last would have made it more likely to be discovered. He dropped the pleading and picked up the phone.

"Jessica Edwards," she answered in her calm, confident voice.

"Jess, it's Dave." Then right to it. "What the hell is this motion *in limine* you filed?"

A slight pause. Long enough to smile, Brunelle knew, even if he couldn't see it. "Which one?" she asked sweetly.

"You know damn well which one," Brunelle replied, definitely not smiling. "The one to exclude any mention of Brown being a pimp or Amy being one of his hookers."

"Oh, right. That one."

Brunelle waited but she didn't say any more. So he did.

"That's total crap, Jess. You know this case only makes sense if the jury knows he was her pimp."

Edwards gave a concerned click of the tongue. "Golly, Dave, I hadn't thought of that. I was just concerned with my client receiving a fair trial. And, you know, the evidence rules are pretty clear: other bad acts aren't generally admissible. A jury might convict him just because they think he's a bad person. The fact that it makes your case incoherent is just a bonus."

"It's not a bonus, it's bullshit. You don't get to gut my case."

"I get to enforce the evidence rules, Dave," Edwards replied, an edge added to her otherwise amiable tone. "And I'm going to advocate on behalf of my client. The jury might make adverse inferences against my client if they know about his other, unrelated criminal activities."

"They're not unrelated, Jess. They're the core of his relationship to the victim."

"Alleged victim," Edwards shot back. "That's motion *in limine* number twelve. You shouldn't get to say 'victim'; you should have to say 'alleged victim.'"

"God, you filed that old motion, too?" Brunelle huffed. "I hate that one. The judges never grant it."

"Grissom might," Edwards replied. "And if she does, you better hope none of your cops slip up and say 'victim' or I'm gonna object and the judge is going to tell the jury that Amy Corrigan is only an 'alleged victim.' Nothing like having the judge broadcast reasonable doubt to the jury."

"Which is why she should deny the motion," Brunelle said. "And the one about Brown being a pimp."

"Look, I bet he'd plead to pimping if you dump the murder charge. You want him to be a pimp, then let's do that and we can both forget about having to try this stupid case."

"It's not a stupid case, Jess."

"You don't have a body, Dave. It's the definition of reasonable doubt." She mocked her closing argument voice, "The judge has instructed you that a reasonable doubt is a doubt for which there is a reason. Ladies and gentleman, what more reason do you need to doubt than the fact that you don't know if Amy Corrigan is even dead?' See, Dave? Stupid."

"She's dead, Jess," Brunelle insisted. "And she's dead because Brown was her pimp and she defied him. The jury needs to know that."

"I agree, Dave," Edwards replied, the overly sweet voice returning. "They will need to know that to convict. That's why I'm going to convince Judge Grissom to exclude it. And you're going to lose."

"We'll see," Brunelle replied. A lame response, he knew, but the first one that came to mind. "I get a chance to argue, too."

"Of course you do, Dave," Edwards almost laughed. "So by all means, tell it to the judge. Judge Grissom, that is."

Brunelle closed his eyes and felt his heart burn as he began imagining Grissom's likely ruling.

"Good bye, Dave," Edwards finished their conversation. "See you in court."

Brunelle didn't reply. He just listened to the click on the other end of the line, then pressed the receiver against his forehead.

"Damn it."

CHAPTER 27

One week before trial, Brunelle walked into Judge Grissom's courtroom for the hearing on Edwards' motions *in limine*. It was also a general status conference to confirm everyone's readiness for trial, and Brunelle had his own motions *in limine* as well, of course, but the thing that really mattered was Edwards' motions. And, specifically, the motion to scrub his case clean of the one thing that allowed it all to make sense.

He wasn't feeling much like small talk, so he avoided his usual nod and greeting to Edwards. His mind was too preoccupied with his upcoming argument, and his heart was too worried about the potential ruling. And if he were honest with himself, he was angry with her. He knew Edwards had to do her job, but that didn't mean he had to like it. And sometimes he just couldn't stuff all the emotions inside any more.

"Good morning, Dave," Edwards tried from her spot at the defense table. Brown was there too, but, as usual, he faded into the background. Just some guy sitting there in a suit looking for all the world to be Edwards' associate rather than a woman-beating pimp and murderer. And, if Edwards got her way, the jury would never get the see the real Kenny Brown.

Brunelle managed to look over and offer a nod in return, but he kept his words to himself and sat down at the prosecution table to arrange his books and binders and notepads.

Edwards didn't press it and sat down as well. The two lawyers readied themselves in silence until Judge Grissom's bailiff announced her arrival.

"All rise," he called. "The King County Superior Court is now in session, the Honorable Helen Grissom presiding."

Grissom ascended to the bench, and Brunelle's heart descended to his stomach. He didn't have a cutesy angle this time. And even if he had, Grissom wasn't likely to be impressed twice by his boyish charm.

"Please be seated," Grissom said as she did the same. "Are the parties ready on the matter of the State of Washington versus Kenneth Wayne Brown?"

Brunelle had remained standing, knowing he would be asked exactly that question and he would be expected to respond first. "The state is ready."

He sat down as Edwards stood up. "The defense is ready," she announced.

And they were off.

Grissom opened the court file before her and thumbed through the top several pages. "We are on for the status conference. Trial is in one week, so I'll start with the obvious question." She raised her eyes to Brunelle. "Is the state ready for trial?"

Brunelle stood again. "Yes, Your Honor."

Grissom looked to Edwards. "Is the defense ready for trial?"

Edwards also stood to address the court. "The defense is ready, Your Honor."

"Good," Grissom replied. "Then I'd like to take the time to

discuss how I run jury selection in my courtroom. I believe it's the standard method, but that's what all the judges say and we each do it a little differently. So, first, we'll bring in a panel of seventy potential jurors—I think that's enough to seat twelve jurors and two alternates. Next, we'll have the first twelve sit in the jury box, then starting with number thirteen, they'll be seated in the gallery…"

Grissom continued on with the basics of jury selection. While it was true each judge did it a little differently, the truth was they all did it basically the same with slight style differences. Brunelle had picked over a hundred juries. He could figure out Grissom's stylistic preferences as they went along. Ordinarily, he might have been able to focus on what she was saying, but he was eager to get to the important stuff: Edwards' motion to gut his case. He had little patience for procedural trivialities.

"Any questions about that procedure, Mr. Brunelle?" the judge asked.

Brunelle knew to look up when his name was mentioned. "No, Your Honor. No questions."

Edwards didn't have any questions either. She'd probably picked more juries than him.

"So, next we can discuss scheduling," Judge Grissom suggested. "Court will begin promptly at nine a.m. every morning and run until noon. After lunch…"

Again, Brunelle found it hard to concentrate. In truth, they would routinely start late because a witness, or juror, or even attorney got caught in traffic. And they would run into the lunch hour as often as not, depending on which witness was on the stand, and whether they were almost done with their testimony, and whether they were even available to come back after lunch.

"Mr. Brunelle?" Judge Grissom was looking down at him.

He refocused his eyes and looked up at the judge. "Yes,

Your Honor?"

"Will that schedule work for you?"

"Uh, yes." Brunelle nodded. Even if he didn't care, he should at least keep listening. "That will be fine. Whatever works for the court, Your Honor. Thank you, Your Honor."

Grissom frowned. She wasn't stupid. "Is there something else you'd like to discuss, Mr. Brunelle?"

Brunelle shrugged slightly. He might as well say it, since she'd bothered to ask. "Could we move on to the motions *in limine*? I think Ms. Edwards and I will be able to adjust to whatever procedural and scheduling demands the court makes on us."

Grissom's frown softened slightly. She was an experienced judge. Brunelle and Edwards were experienced attorneys. The day-to-day details would work themselves out. What really mattered right then was what the judge's legal rulings would be. Brunelle could easily show up to Grissom's courtroom at 9:00 a.m. every day. What he really cared about was what he was going to be allowed to talk about when he got there.

"Okay, Mr. Brunelle," the judge replied. She looked to the defense table. "Are you ready to address the motions *in limine,* Ms. Edwards?"

Edwards nodded. "Yes, Your Honor. Whatever the court wants to do."

Grissom nodded. "Fine. Shall we start with the state's motions?"

It was normal practice to start everything with the prosecution's side of the argument. That whole presumption of innocence, burden of proof thing. But Brunelle wasn't sure he could make it through his own formulaic motions to exclude witnesses from the courtroom during other witnesses' testimony, etc. "Could we start with the defense motions, Your Honor?" he suggested. "I think they're more… substantial."

Grissom smiled slightly at Brunelle. A knowing smile. Unlike Judge Carlisle, she had undoubtedly read all of the pleadings. And having done so, she would have known what Brunelle was most concerned about. Brunelle realized the discussion about jury selection procedures and lunch times may have been a bit of Grissom toying with him—like a cat with an injured bird.

"I assume you don't mean Ms. Edwards' motion to prevent your witnesses from using the word 'victim'?" she ventured.

Brunelle grimaced. "I do want to be heard on that motion too, Your Honor. But no. I'm chiefly concerned with her motion *in limine* number seventeen, asking the court to exclude any mention of the defendant's criminal activities in promoting prostitution."

Grissom's cat-like smile broadened just a bit. She looked to Edwards. "Are you ready to argue that motion right now, counsel?"

Edwards smiled as well. Brunelle felt like the guy in the room who wasn't in on the joke. "Yes, Your Honor. Whatever you say."

Grissom leaned back slightly. She exchanged the smile for a thoughtful expression and clasped her hands in front of her. "This is your motion, Ms. Edwards. You may begin."

"Thank you, Your Honor," Edwards replied.

Brunelle, who had been standing to address the court, sat down again and listened intently to Edwards, pen in his hand to write down her major points—and the responses he would offer when it was his turn to speak.

"The defense asks the court to exclude any allegation, argument, testimony, or other mention that Mr. Brown has ever engaged in the crime of promoting prostitution. The motion is made pursuant to evidence rules 403, 404, and 609. As the court is aware,

Rule 404(b) states clearly that," Edwards looked down to her rule book to quote verbatim, "'Evidence of other crimes, wrongs, or acts is not admissible to prove the character of a person in order to show action in conformity therewith.' Here, the state would be introducing the evidence to argue that Mr. Brown is a pimp and this is the sort of things pimps do."

Brunelle frowned. That wasn't exactly what he would be arguing. But he knew not to interrupt.

"In addition," Edwards continued, "evidence rule 609 limits evidence of criminal activity to crimes of dishonesty, like perjury. It states, in pertinent part, 'For the purpose of attacking the credibility of a witness in a criminal or civil case, evidence that the witness has been convicted of a crime shall be admitted ... but only if the crime ... involved dishonesty or false statement.' Here, the allegations of pimping are not crimes of dishonesty and so should be excluded."

Brunelle suppressed a shake of his head. That was for using old convictions to suggest a witness was a liar, not new criminal activity that was relevant to the current charges.

So, likely knowing what Brunelle would argue, Edwards finished with, "And even if the court thinks there may be some minimal relevance of the pimping allegations, evidence rule 403 clearly states, 'Although relevant, evidence may be excluded if its probative value is substantially outweighed by the danger of unfair prejudice, confusion of the issues, or misleading the jury.' Here, there would be a great danger that the jury, hearing that Mr. Brown may have acted as a pimp to some women who worked as prostitutes, would label him as simply a 'bad man' and convict him because of that label, even if the evidence is insufficient to establish his guilt beyond a reasonable doubt as to the crime charged. This is especially true in a case such as this where the state insists on pressing forward with a circumstantial case, not even having proof that the victim is actually dead."

'Alleged' victim, Brunelle thought to himself sardonically.

"Therefore, Your Honor," Edwards concluded, "the defense urges the court to exclude any reference to alleged pimping activities by Mr. Brown and require the state to proceed based on what little evidence they have and not on insinuations and innuendo. Thank you."

Brunelle stood up as Judge Grissom turned her attention to him. "Response?"

"Yes, Your Honor. Thank you." Brunelle straightened his suit and looked down at the first point on his legal pad. "To begin with, Your Honor, the state is not seeking to introduce the evidence to establish any sort of character of Mr. Brown. We aren't trying to say he's a certain type of person and people like that would commit murder. Ms. Edwards left off the last sentence of evidence rule 404(b), which states quite clearly, that evidence of other crimes, wrongs, or acts, 'may, however, be admissible for other purposes, such as proof of motive.' Here, the motive for the murder was a prostitute who disrespected and disobeyed her pimp. That's not inadmissible propensity evidence; it's admissible evidence of motive."

Brunelle felt like he'd articulated that rebuttal to Edwards' first argument rather well. He looked down to his next note. "As far as evidence rule 609 goes, the court knows that rule only governs the admissibility of prior convictions when cross-examining a witness. The pimping activity here is contemporaneous with the murder, not some years-old conviction for perjury or false swearing. We are not seeking to admit it under 609, so 609 doesn't control whether it's admissible or not."

Brunelle nodded, again pleased with his oratory.

"Essentially, Your Honor, the relationship between Mr.

Brown and the victim, Amy Corrigan, is integral to the state's theory of the case. As such, it is admissible to show motive and to explain to the jury the entire dynamic between the parties. Accordingly, Ms. Edwards' motion *in limine* should be denied. Thank you."

Brunelle expected Grissom to turn back to Edwards for the defense attorney's rebuttal, but instead she kept her gaze on Brunelle. "What about Ms. Edwards' 403 argument? That even if it's relevant, it should be excluded as overly prejudicial."

Brunelle kept a poker face. Or rather a lawyer face, manufacturing an expression of interest but calm. Not betraying the panic that shot into his heart at the judge giving any credence to that argument. Defense attorneys always cited 403. It was the last gasp of a desperate litigator. 'Sure,' the argument went, 'it's relevant and otherwise admissible, but please keep it out anyway, because it just hurts my case so dang much.'

"Well, I think it's important to note that rule 403 presupposes relevance," Brunelle began. "And that's important, because the evidence is relevant. It's very relevant. Next, the rule doesn't allow relevant evidence to be excluded just because there might be some prejudice to its admission. That prejudice has to, not just outweigh, but *substantially* outweigh the probative value. Here, the probative value is to paint for the jury the full picture of these two people, how their lives are entwined, and how that could lead to the violent death of one of them. Finally, the prejudice to be avoided isn't just any prejudice, but unfair prejudice. So, the court has to ask itself, is it unfair for the jury to hear the truth about Mr. Brown? And I would argue that the truth is never unfair. The court should deny the motion."

Grissom chewed her cheek for several seconds, keeping her eyes locked with Brunelle's then she tore them away to address

Edwards. "Any rebuttal, Ms. Edwards?"

Edwards smiled. Her own version of lawyer-face. "Yes, Your Honor. Mr. Brunelle's response belies his true intent. He claims the truth is never unfair, but what truth, and told by whom? The mere allegation that Mr. Brown was a pimp is enough to smear him beyond redemption in the eyes of the jury. That is substantial and that is unfair. Mr. Brunelle should have to prove his case based on the facts surrounding the murder, not ancillary allegations of unrelated criminal activity. He can present a sanitized version of his case, mentioning that Mr. Brown and Ms. Corrigan were known to each other, but leaving out the full nature of their acquaintance. That would be fair and that's what the court should require."

Grissom nodded and looked back to Brunelle. "What about that, Mr. Brunelle? You can tell the jury that they knew each other, maybe even that Ms. Corrigan worked for Mr. Brown, but you can't say anything about pimping or prostitution? That sounds fair."

But Brunelle shook his head. "No, Your Honor. With all due respect, that sounds ludicrous. The jury will assume Amy was his secretary or something—especially with him sitting there in a suit—and there's no rational basis to expect a businessman would murder his secretary for no reason."

"Are you commenting on Mr. Brown's right to be dressed in street clothes, Mr. Brunelle?" Judge Grissom demanded. "He posted bail and can wear whatever he wants. Even if he hadn't posted bail, he'd still be dressed in street clothes for the jury so they wouldn't know he was in custody. I, for one, appreciate that his attire shows respect for this court and these proceedings."

Fuck, Brunelle thought. He'd pissed off the judge. That was never good.

"That's not what I meant, Your Honor," he defended. "I simply meant that juries tend to fill in details, and if they don't know the whole story, they might jump to erroneous conclusions."

"Like the notion that pimps are bad," Grissom challenged, "and bad people murder people?"

Brunelle inclined his head slowly. "No," he said carefully. "Just that Mr. Brown knew Ms. Corrigan, was Ms. Corrigan's pimp, and killed Ms. Corrigan."

Grissom narrowed her eyes. "Say that sentence again, except replace the word 'pimp' with the word 'boss.'"

Brunelle bristled. But he knew to follow an order from a judge. "Mr. Brown knew Ms. Corrigan. He was Ms. Corrigan's *boss*. And he killed Ms. Corrigan."

"There," the judge said. "Why can't you just say that?"

"Because it isn't true," Brunelle protested.

"He wasn't her boss?" Grissom questioned.

Brunelle shrugged slightly, although his body remained tense. "In a way, but not the way the jury will think when they hear 'boss' instead of 'pimp.' It's not just that they had some sort of business relationship. It's the nature of that relationship. Him being her pimp is the whole thing. It's the, the..." He searched for the right phrase. "It's all part of the *res gestae*."

Brunelle felt his heart drop. Latin was never a good thing to throw around. It was usually employed to cover cracks in one's logic, like spackling. And '*res gestae*' was the worst Latin phrase there was. It translated literally as 'things done' or 'deed.' So really, you were just saying, 'It should be admitted because it's part of it.' Brunelle recalled a law professor who told the class that claiming evidence was '*res gestae*' was the last thing an advocate tried when they were about to lose the argument. Brunelle knew this would be no exception to that rule.

"*Res gestae*?" Judge Grissom repeated. "Well, yes, it is part of the *res gestae*. Everything is part of the *res gestae*. That's sort of what *res gestae* means. And then there are a hundred evidence rules designed to restrict and exclude those parts of the *res gestae* that shouldn't be admitted. Hearsay, insurance coverage, prior criminal history. All those things are part of every case's *res gestae*—and then judges exclude it all because it would be unfair to just let everything in."

"Because juries can't be trusted?" Brunelle snapped. He was getting frustrated. Never good for a trial attorney.

"Because criminal defendants have a right to a fair trial," Grissom corrected testily.

Brunelle didn't reply. He didn't trust what might come out of his mouth. Edwards was silent too, but it was the silence of a victor. Trying not to rock the boat as it coasted toward the finish line.

"I'm going to grant the motion *in limine*," Grissom declared. "You are permitted to describe Mr. Brown's and Ms. Corrigan's relationship as one of employer and employee, but you can't describe it as pimping or prostitution."

"Just another girl from the typing pool, huh?" Brunelle quipped darkly.

The judge didn't appear to appreciate the joke. "Do you understand my ruling, Mr. Brunelle?"

Brunelle submitted a begrudging nod. "Yes, Your Honor."

"Any questions about it?" Grissom pressed.

Brunelle was about to say, 'No, Your Honor,' but then he thought of something. "So I can talk about the entire business enterprise? As long as I don't call it pimping or prostitution?"

Grissom hesitated, squinting down at Brunelle with wary eyes. "Yes," she said carefully.

"And I can talk about the other girls in the typing pool?"

Judge Grissom crossed her arms. "As long as you don't tell

the jury they're prostitutes."

"Okay," Brunelle agreed. "I'll just tell them that another girl from the typing pool died after she crossed good ol' Mr. Brown."

Grissom's arms fell uncrossed and she leaned forward sharply. "A prostitute?"

"Oh, no, Your Honor," Brunelle replied with an exaggerated wave. "No prostitutes here. Just another girl from the typing pool. Apparently, working for Mr. Brown is a dangerous line of work."

Grissom's nostrils flared. "Did she also disappear, Mr. Brunelle?"

"No, no, Your Honor," Brunelle answered cheerily, ignoring the judge's tone. "She OD'd in the motel room the defendant rented for her so she could, uh, type."

Grissom didn't react angrily. Instead, she tapped her fingers on the bench. "And how would that be relevant to anything at issue in this case?"

"Well," Brunelle answered, gaining some confidence in the judge's reaction to his admittedly sarcastic suggestion, "it goes to show that Mr. Brown's, uh, 'business' isn't all love and roses, so to speak. That it's dangerous to work for Mr. Brown. In fact," Brunelle slapped his forehead in faux epiphany, "she died the very night you, Your Honor, ordered me to provide her name to Mr. Brown's attorney. What a crazy coincidence, huh?"

Judge Grissom glared down at Brunelle with furrowed brow and piercing eyes, but she didn't immediately find words. Brunelle knew that, as a judge, she was angry at his disrespect. But he also knew, as a human being, she would be bothered that someone may have died, at least in part, because of her.

"May I be heard, Your Honor?" Edwards spoke up.

Grissom rotated her head toward Edwards, but held her eyes on Brunelle until the last possible moment. "Yes, Ms.

Edwards?"

"I would object to this evidence," Edwards said calmly, her professionalism contrasting Brunelle's flippancy. "First, it's not relevant to the case at bar. Second, this is the first I've heard of it. I don't have any autopsy reports or anything, and trial starts in one week."

Grissom raised an eyebrow at Edwards. "Is this really the first time Mr. Brunelle mentioned it to you?"

Edwards shifted her weight. "Well, this is the first I heard he intended to introduce it at trial. He did mention it to me right after it happened."

"I'm sure he did," the judge muttered. Then, in a louder voice, "So you've been aware of this for some time now?"

Edwards' face contorted as she considered the best way to reply. "Yes, Your Honor," she finally admitted.

Grissom leaned back and steepled her fingers. The attorneys remained silent as she considered her decision. After several more seconds, she leaned forward and spoke. "I'm going to give you a choice, Ms. Edwards. Option one is, I exclude all mention of pimping and prostitution but I allow evidence of the other witness's death. Option two is, I exclude the second death, but Mr. Brunelle can tell the jury that the alleged victim was a prostitute and your client was her pimp."

Edwards blinked up at the judge. Grissom was patient as Edwards weighed her options. And Brunelle knew to shut up while she decided.

"Thank you, Your Honor," Edwards finally responded. "I'll take option number one. I still object to any discussion of the other woman's death, but given the choice as the court has framed it, I believe option one is the best for my client."

Brunelle couldn't disagree. Edwards hadn't taken the bait.

His gambit had been to get Grissom to change her ruling and allow in evidence of the pimping. That had failed. And although getting to talk about Linda's death might help, even when scrubbed of any mention of pimping and prostitution, there was a downside.

He had to call Kat as a witness.

CHAPTER 28

Brunelle knew he couldn't just send Kat a subpoena through the mail. Well, actually, he could do that, but he knew he shouldn't. For one thing, it was cowardly. More importantly, she'd call him anyway to ask why the hell he'd sent her a subpoena.

He tasked Nicole with ordering Linda's autopsy report from the medical examiner staff and forwarding it on to Edwards. But the explanation to the witness of what testimony was expected, that fell on the trial attorney.

So he called Kat's office number. He didn't call her private cell number—which was still in his phone contacts—because it was work-related. And because when he called after nine o'clock at night, she might answer her cell phone, but her office phone would go straight to voicemail.

Cowardly, but effectively so.

'Hello. You've reached the voicemail of Dr. Kat Anderson of the King County Medical Examiner's Office. Please leave me a message and I'll call you back as soon as I can.'

Beep!

"Oh, hey, Kat. It's Dave. Uh, Brunelle. I was just calling to let you know I'll be sending you a subpoena about the Linda Prescott autopsy. Uh, the judge is gonna let me talk about it. A bit. Kinda. Well, it's sorta complicated. I can't really mention the whole prostitute thing. But yeah, anyway, I just need you to tell the jury that she O.D.'d. I won't ask you to say homicide. I promise." He immediately regretted saying that; he didn't have a good record of keeping his promises to her. "Uh, right. Okay, well anyway, um, I hope you're doing well. And Lizzy, too." Ugh, why did he say that? He needed to hang up. "Okay, sorry. Uh, no need to call back. I just wanted to let you know about the subpoena. I'll have Nicole call you about scheduling. Okay. Uh, bye."

Brunelle hung up and ran a hand through his graying hair. His heart was racing. And aching.

Cowardly, and poorly executed. Perfect combination.

He needed to do better with the last subpoena. There was no room for cowardice. And poor execution could cost him a lot more than temporary mortification.

CHAPTER 29

Brunelle eventually realized that he should have brought Chen with him again. Not when he first arrived at the Aurora Motel, but definitely by the time he left. And not because it was always good to have a witness to a subpoena being served.

Again, Brunelle came at night. Not because he particularly wanted to be at a hooker hotel after dark, but because that was when he was going to be able to find Jillian Hammond, a.k.a. 'Tina.' And he wasn't about to try to schedule another date via text, à la Linda Prescott. So, just like the first time he'd gone trolling for a hooker, he pulled into the hotel parking lot alone and drove slowly to a parking spot in the back.

But unlike that time, Jillian didn't walk up to his car. No one did. Brunelle had noticed some probable prostitutes loitering near the driveway, but none bothered to follow him in into the lot. He waited for what seemed like forever—but was likely no more than a long minute—then opened his car door and stepped into the cool Seattle night.

There were a few people out and about, besides Brunelle and the prostitutes. Three guys were outside their first-floor room, leaning against a beat-up car and smoking. There was an overweight woman walking toward the manager's office. And there was a toddler screaming somewhere. Brunelle walked away from the sound of the wailing child toward the image of the plying women, vaguely aware and mildly nauseated by the biological connection between them. No wonder he'd never had kids.

There was one prostitute on the left side of the driveway. It wasn't Jillian. Too tall. To the right were three or four more and Jillian could have been hidden among them; it was hard to tell in the dark. He slowed his approach and craned his neck slightly to see around the large woman with her back to him.

"Hey there, handsome." One of them had spied him. Again, though, it wasn't Jillian. "You looking for a date?"

She stepped out from the herd and toward Brunelle. She was average height, skinny, with bleached platinum hair teased up on top of her head. What clothes she wore were designed to come off easily and look like they would.

"Uh, maybe," Brunelle answered. "I'm looking for Tina."

The woman smiled, although there was a bit of snarl hidden in it. No one likes to lose a sale. "Tina, huh?" She looked back to the other women. "He likes 'em small and thick." Then, turning back to Brunelle, "Sure you don't want to try something long and lean?"

Brunelle was sure. "Uh, sorry, no. Just looking for Tina. Is she around?"

The woman frowned at being rejected but then shrugged. There'd be business enough for her that night, Brunelle supposed. She turned back to her group. "Didn't Tina drive off with that fat guy in the pickup truck?"

Brunelle couldn't help but wince. On his previous visits—and certainly when Chen actually accused him of it—he'd considered what it might be like to have sex with a prostitute. He'd found the thought unappealing, for many reasons. But he hadn't fully realized what it must be like for the women to get into a car with some stranger whose appearance, personality, and hygiene might all be unpleasant, or worse.

"Yeah," one of the women replied. "But she'll be back any second. That guy never lasts."

The other women laughed and murmured in knowing agreement. A few moment later, true to prediction, the beat-up pickup truck pulled into the parking lot, driving over the curb as it did so, and came to an abrupt stop near them. The driver was unkempt, with white hair, a yellow-gray beard, and a fat, flushed face.

Brunelle instinctively looked away, repulsed by the thoughts seeping into his mind against his will. When he turned back, 'Tina' was climbing out of the cab, her short skirt riding up to expose her G-string. If she said anything to the john in departure, Brunelle didn't hear it. She closed the truck door and the truck pulled quickly back onto Aurora Avenue.

"Hey there, Tina!" said the long and lean woman. "You're up again." She pointed at Brunelle. "This guy asked for you special."

Brunelle could feel his own face flush, and was glad for the cover the evening darkness gave him. This was not how he'd wanted this to go down. The plan was to find her, slip her the subpoena, and leave. Now he had an audience.

Jillian/Tina didn't seem any happier about it. "Oh," was all she managed to say. That just made it all the more awkward.

"Uh, my car is over there," Brunelle tried, nodding toward the back of the lot. It was looking like he'd have to do another fake date. Drive her to a park, give her the subpoena, plus enough cash to keep her pimp from getting curious. The problem was, he hadn't brought a fistful of cash with him this time, just the subpoena. If he could just get her away from the other women, he could hand her the subpoena and get out of there. She could tell them he'd chickened out or something and they could all laugh at him while he drove away.

'Tina' didn't respond. She just stood there, her expression guarded. It got strangely tense as the other women tried to figure out why Tina wasn't walking to her next trick. Finally, she smiled tightly and said, "Okay."

Brunelle breathed a sigh of relief and turned to lead the way to his car. He didn't want to walk right next to her, although he wasn't exactly sure why. He decided not to question the instinct; it was likely way too complicated.

When they got far enough away from the other women, Tina grabbed his arm and spun him around to face her. "What the hell are you doing here? Do you want to get us both killed?"

Brunelle very much did not want that. "I just need to give you a subpoena."

If Tina had looked surprised to see him when she climbed out of the pickup, she looked absolutely dumbfounded at Brunelle's comment. "A subpoena?" she whispered. She glanced around frantically. "Are you fucking kidding me? I told you I wouldn't testify."

Brunelle nodded. "Exactly. That's why I need to give you the subpoena. If I thought you'd come voluntarily, I wouldn't have to. But I need you to testify and so I need to get you under subpoena."

They had stopped well short of his car. And now they were arguing. Not exactly inconspicuous. The three smoking guys were looking at them. And that damn toddler was still screaming. A motel room door opened nearby.

"And where the hell am I supposed to put your subpoena

where my pimp don't find it?" Tina demanded. "He checks everything." Then, to make sure Brunelle understood, she patted her crotch and repeated, "Everything."

Brunelle lowered his gaze. He hadn't thought of that. Then again, it really didn't matter if she kept it, just that he'd given it to her. She could throw it out as soon as he handed it to her. He told her as much.

"Oh, Okay." Tina threw her hands up in the air. "I'll just toss it into the nearest trash can where anyone can find it and show everyone around here that I'm a snitch."

Brunelle put out a reassuring hand. "Look, Jillian— "

"Don't call me that!" she shouted. "Don't ever call me that. I'm Tina. When I'm working, I'm Tina." Then she sighed ever so slightly. "And I'm always working."

"This guy being a problem, Tina?" That nearby door that had opened had produced two very large men, not necessarily in height, but definitely in muscles. They were both in their early 20s. One wore a tank-top, the other a tight t-shirt. Both modes of dress showed off their massive arms and chests, extensively tattooed and rippling with aggression.

"Yeah," Tina answered with an evil smile. "This fucker said he doesn't have any money on him."

The man in the tank-top squared his shoulders to Brunelle and stepped toward him. "I ain't running no fucking charity, douche bag. You can't pay, you can't play." He looked at Tina. "You already do the date?"

She shook her head. "No, I was walking to his car when he asked if I'd do it for free this time. He said he could go to the ATM afterwards."

Brunelle raised his palms and took a step backward. "I don't want any trouble."

"Well, that's too bad, 'cause you found it," the main pimp answered. The other one, the one in the t-shirt, stayed back closer to the motel room. Tina stepped over to him and he put his arm round her waist; they watched as Brunelle tried to extricate himself from the situation. "You don't fuck with T-Jo," the angry man in Brunelle's face warned through gritted teeth. "You don't rip off T-Jo."

At least Brunelle would know the name of the man who killed him. Well, his street name anyway. "Look, I wasn't trying to rip anybody off," Brunelle insisted. "It was just a misunderstanding."

"Misunderstanding?" T-Jo said. "What don't you understand? You wanna fuck her, you pay her first. Ain't nothing to misunderstand."

"Well, right," Brunelle replied. "That's just it. I wasn't actually trying to, uh, fuck her..."

T-Jo narrowed his eyes. "You into some kinky shit or something? Man, I don't care if you wanna suck her toes or have her hit you with a belt or whatever. You fucking pay first. What you do after that, I don't give a fuck."

"Right, right," Brunelle agreed. He was only a few feet from his car. If he could just end the conversation with all of his bones unbroken. "Sure. Like I said, just a misunderstanding. I'll just be going. Sorry about all this. Really. Sorry."

But before he could turn away, T-Jo grabbed his arm. "Wait a second. You aren't into that shit. That ain't why you're here." He looked Brunelle up and down. "You one of those fucking do-gooders from that church, ain't ya? Trying to talk my girls outta making a good living for themselves."

There was so much wrong with that statement. He wasn't a do-gooder. He definitely wasn't from any church. And there was no way Tina was a making a good living—she was giving all her money to T-Jo in exchange for a motel room and some drugs. So Brunelle provided the only rational response, given the situation.

"Yes," he lied. "That's it exactly. Sorry to waste everyone's time. I'll just leave now and never come back."

Brunelle slipped his arm out of T-Jo's grip and turned to walk, as quickly as he could without actually running, to his car. He thought he'd pulled off the escape. But just as he reached the vehicle, T-Jo grabbed his arm again—twisting it behind his back and driving his face into the car door.

"Now you listen up and you listen good," T-Jo growled in his ear. "You leave my girls alone. You leave all these girls alone. They don't want your help, man. I give 'em a place to stay and food to eat. That's better than most of their parents ever did for 'em. And what the fuck are you offering? A fucking prayer card and a care package with some soap? You gonna let her sleep at your house? You gonna let her meet your fucking kids? I don't think so." He pushed Brunelle's face back against the car window. "So you get the fuck out of here and never, ever fucking come back. And consider yourself lucky you didn't end up with a bullet in your ass."

Brunelle nodded but didn't say anything. Discretion was the better part of valor, or something like that. Shutting up was the most likely chance of getting out of there without further injury. T-Jo released his arm and shoved him one last time into the car door. Brunelle kept his eyes down and scrambled into his car as fast as he could. He tore out of the parking lot even faster and was a good three miles up Aurora Avenue before he felt his pulse start to slow.

CHAPTER 30

In a profession like trial lawyer, which involved a unique blend of intimate public speaking and subtle salesmanship, there were certain advantages to being a man or woman, depending on the type of case and the role of the lawyer. If you're charged with a sex offense, you might want a female attorney at your side; just a subtle suggestion that you're not a complete reprobate.

One benefit of being a man was that graying hair and a fading bruise on your cheek just made you look wise and tough. Brunelle was able to show up on the morning of trial looking seasoned, rugged, ready for battle. The same gray hair and facial injury would have made Edwards look haggard and potentially abused. Like she'd gone out for a middle-aged roller derby team.

Still, one person's rugged was another person's ugly.

"What the hell happened to you?" Edwards asked when she saw him. "You look like hell."

"My car ran into something," Brunelle answered as he set his trial briefcase on the table and undid its clasps.

"What did it run into?" Edwards asked.

Brunelle extracted his evidence handbook and finally looked

at Edwards. He managed a smile. "My face."

Edwards raised an eyebrow but before she could ask further, Judge Grissom took the bench.

"Are we ready to pick the jury?" she inquired as she settled into her judge's chair.

Edwards was first to respond. "Yes, Your Honor," she answered brightly.

Brunelle looked up at the judge and shrugged. His cheek still stung a little. "Sure, Your Honor. Why not?"

* * *

The thing about jury selection is that it's really jury de-selection. Potential jurors think they're going to be affirmatively chosen for the jury but, in fact, the exact opposite is true. Each side gets to strike six potential jurors from the panel, and the first twelve of whoever's left are the jury. The best way to get out of serving on a jury was to talk a lot during the questioning. Have lots of opinions and you're sure to make one side or the other not want you on the jury. Don't like cops? The prosecutor will strike you. Figure a defendant must have done something to get arrested? The defense attorney will strike you.

As a result, a jury ends up being the twelve people with the least personality, or the best ability to cover it up. A blank slate of retired aviation workers and teachers whose contract pays them even when they're on jury duty. Twelve people with weak enough opinions that the lawyers think they might be able to persuade them with profound oratory and flashy PowerPoint slides. Twelve people sworn to return 'a true and proper verdict.' Twelve people who, once so sworn, and after the lawyers got a quick break to clear their heads and switch gears, were instructed by Judge Grissom, "Now, ladies and gentlemen, please give your attention to Mr. Brunelle who will deliver the opening statement on behalf of the state."

CHAPTER 31

Brunelle stood up, thanked the judge, and turned his attention to the people in the jury box—ignoring the people in the gallery, and remembering the one person the case was really about.

"Amy Corrigan," he began. His voice was a bit scratchy on this first effort, so he repeated himself. "Amy Corrigan. You're going to hear from a lot of witnesses during this trial, but the one person you won't hear from is the most important person in the case. Amy Corrigan. Because Amy Corrigan is dead."

Brunelle paused just a beat, then pointed at the defense table to say, "And Kenny Brown murdered her."

Okay, good start, Brunelle thought. But the jurors already knew that. The judge had told them it was a murder trial. Brown had been identified as the defendant. That meant somebody was dead, and the defendant was accused of making them that way. What they didn't know was who, or why, or how. Brunelle couldn't answer the 'how,' but he was pretty sure about the 'why,' and he was going to hammer on the 'who.'

"Before I tell you what happened to Amy the night she was murdered, let me tell you about her before she was murdered. Let me tell you about what she was like when she was alive. Sometimes, here in these nice courtrooms," he paused to gesture vaguely around the room, "with their polished wood and crisp, new flags, we can forget about the real world. About real people, and the real situations they find themselves in, and the real choices they make." Another deliberate pause. Then, "And the all too real consequences of those choices."

So that completed the set up. Brunelle took a step to the side, signaling a shift in the narrative, and clasped his hands together loosely in front of him.

"Amy Corrigan," again with her name, "grew up right here in King County. In SeaTac, just south of Burien and—like everyone else who lived in a town named after an airport—directly in the flight path of SeaTac International Airport. She grew up being able to ignore the monsters looming overhead each day." Another glance toward Brown. "It was a skill that would serve her well in later life."

Brunelle mentally tensed, awaiting the possible objection from Edwards. But she was too good of a trial lawyer to take the bait. Some defense attorneys objected during prosecution openings just to disrupt the rhythm, but Brunelle's experience had been that whatever benefit there may have been in that, it was usually outweighed by the irritation felt by jurors at having their attention interrupted. 'Just wait your turn' was the expression most jurors wore after the second or third such objection. Brunelle was testing her with the 'monster' comment. He wanted to see how far he could push. Pretty far, apparently, but that just meant Edwards was that confident in her own opening statement.

"Amy was like anyone else," Brunelle continued. "She struggled to make her way in the world as she grew up, rebelling against parents and experimenting with what the world had to offer, good and bad."

Brunelle wasn't sure how much she had rebelled, actually, but ending up a drug-addicted prostitute probably wasn't on her parents' short list of life wishes for their daughter.

"Eventually she found her way to the defendant, Kenneth Brown." Another glance toward the defense table, except this time, everyone in the room did it. Brown looked up from his legal pad long enough to recognize the mention of his name, then looked down again. Edwards had cleaned him up really well. He was in a dark suit, white shirt, muted tie. Fresh haircut and no jewelry. No one would ever guess he was a pimp and a murderer. Brunelle frowned at the sight.

"He offered her a job," Brunelle turned back to the jury and continued. "And a place to stay. But there was a catch. There's always a catch. She had to give all her money to Mr. Brown, and she stayed where he said. And did whatever he said."

Edwards stood up at that. "Objection, Your Honor."

Brunelle's eyebrows knitted together. He looked up at Judge Grissom. He hadn't used any inflammatory language and had avoided the word 'pimp,' rather artfully, he thought. "What's the objection, Your Honor?"

Grissom looked down at Edwards. "The objection, counselor?"

Edwards hesitated. "Could I be heard outside the presence of the jury?"

Brunelle suppressed an eye roll. He was wrong about her not wanting to interrupt his flow. Nothing could be more disruptive than to stop his presentation and take the jury back to the jury room for five or ten minutes while the attorneys argued over his choice of words.

"I would object to that, Your Honor," Brunelle said. "I'm in the middle of my opening statement. I believe I know what Ms.

Edwards' concern is, and I can tell the court I have no intention of going there."

"That's just it, Your Honor," Edwards replied. "I think he already has."

Brunelle closed his eyes for a moment in frustration, but then caught himself—he was still in front of the jury. Frustration suggested weakness, a lack of confidence in his case. He took a deep breath and tried to radiate calm confidence as he awaited the judge's decision.

Grissom's expression twisted as she weighed the importance of reining Brunelle in from a fatal mistake against the professionalism of allowing an attorney to do their job unimpeded. Finally, she motioned for the attorneys to come forward. "Sidebar," she announced.

Brunelle shrugged inside. That was probably the best compromise. Admonishment with minimal interruption. He and Edwards stepped up to the edge of the bench, and Grissom leaned down to whisper at them.

"You're getting awfully close to telling the jury he's a pimp," Grissom whispered, anticipating Edwards' complaint.

"He all but did it," Edwards added. "Telling them she had to give all her money to him."

But Brunelle disagreed. "It could be a sweatshop, or housecleaning, or a meat-packing factory. Anything underground. Anything where she's being taken advantage of."

"I let the monsters comments go," Edwards said.

"Your fault, not mine," Brunelle responded.

"Don't." Grissom halted the bickering, giving both of them a hard glare. "Mr. Brunelle, you're getting very close to stepping over the line. Be careful. You cross it, and I won't hesitate to declare a mistrial."

"And I'll file the motion to dismiss for misconduct before her gavel falls," Edwards threatened.

Brunelle smiled coldly at the apparent double team. He'd won the objection after all. He just needed to be careful.

"Understood, Your Honor," he whispered to Grissom. He ignored Edwards' comment. "May I continue now?"

Grissom nodded. "Yes. But move on. I won't do another sidebar."

Brunelle wasn't sure if that meant she'd take the jury out at the next objection, or if she'd just declare the mistrial at that point. He decided it didn't matter. He would just avoid any further objections. Besides, he'd made his point. If there was one thing everyone in the room knew, regardless of whether they were privy to the sidebar, it was that the issue of Amy's 'business relationship' with Kenny Brown was a big deal and the defense didn't like it at all.

Good, Brunelle thought as he retook his place before the jurors.

"As I was saying, Amy Corrigan found Kenneth Brown. Or rather, Kenneth Brown found Amy. But he was no benefactor. In fact, the women who worked for Mr. Brown had a habit of dying under suspicious circumstances."

Edwards stood up again, smacking the table as she did so. "Objection, Your Honor! Now I insist I be heard outside the presence of the jury."

Grissom frowned at Brunelle. He didn't bother arguing against it. Besides, if the sidebar had underlined the 'business relationship' for the jury, then being sent out of the courtroom would underline and highlight the whole 'women had a habit of dying' thing.

"Ladies and Gentleman," Grissom looked to the jury box.

"I'm going to ask you to retire to the jury room for a moment while I discuss a matter with the attorneys. This won't take long. Thank you for your patience."

The jurors stood up and filed out obediently. It was early in the trial still. They hadn't been stuck sitting in uncomfortable chairs for enough days on end yet to grumble at yet another interruption. As soon as the door closed, Brunelle took the offensive.

"I'm very troubled that Ms. Edwards keeps interrupting my opening statement," he complained before the judge could address either attorney. "She'll get her turn to speak."

Edwards jumped in next. "I keep interrupting because you keep violating the pretrial orders. First, you all but tell them Amy was a prostitute and now you tell them people 'have a habit of dying' when they work for my client."

"Which is exactly what I can say," Brunelle countered, "based on the pretrial rulings."

Grissom cleared her throat. "May I be heard?" It wasn't really a question, of course.

She waited for a reply anyway so Brunelle and Edwards were both forced to offer a meek, "Yes, Your Honor."

Grissom smiled for just a moment, then her expression turned to stone. "You," she pointed at Edwards. "Stop objecting. Mr. Brunelle is right on the edge, but he hasn't stepped over it."

Then she pointed at Brunelle. "And you, step away from the edge. Several steps. One slip of your tongue and this case goes down the toilet. If you accidentally say something against my rulings that poisons this jury, I won't just be granting Ms. Edwards' motion for mistrial, I'll be granting her motion to dismiss. Understood?"

Brunelle nodded. "Understood, Your Honor."

The finger swung back to Edwards. "Understood? "

"Yes, Your Honor, " Edwards agreed.

Grissom raised her gaze to the bailiff waiting at the jury room door. "Bring the jury back in," she ordered. "I'm not going to sustain or overrule the objection. Just move on, Mr. Brunelle. Move on."

Brunelle nodded and waited as the bailiff brought the jurors back in. He wished Grissom would have said 'overruled' when they came back in so they would know he hadn't done anything wrong, but Grissom's tone didn't invite argument. He'd just have to be satisfied that Edwards wouldn't interrupt him any more.

"As I was saying," he started up again, trying to reestablish his flow, "Amy Corrigan got herself wrapped up with the defendant, and it was this relationship that ultimately led to her death."

Brunelle paused for a moment. In part to reestablish himself—when a speaker pauses, it reaffirms that the others in the room are the passive party, having to wait for the speaker to continue, something never noticed if the speaker continues uninterrupted. The other reason Brunelle paused was because this was the hardest part of his case to explain. He knew Amy was dead, but exactly how it happened, he didn't have a clue. The weakness in his case. So he would try to make the weakness a strength. And Edwards wasn't allowed to interrupt.

"The saddest part of Amy Corrigan's death is that it was completely anonymous. She just disappeared. There was no dramatic shoot-out in the parking lot, horrified onlookers shrieking. No ambulance speeding to the hospital, lights flashing and siren wailing. No mournful funeral where family and friends could share their memories of her life. And no grave marker, where Amy's two-year-old daughter could say goodbye to her mommy."

Brunelle sensed Edwards tense at his blatant appeal to

emotion, but she kept her objection in check.

"No, the only person who knows exactly what happened to Amy Corrigan is the man who killed her." A final accusatory finger at the defendant. "Kenneth Brown."

Brunelle turned back to the jury and deepened his voice in pitch and force. "The state will call many witnesses in this case. Amy's family. Amy's friends. Amy's coworkers. At the end of this trial, you may not know all the details of Amy's death, but you'll know one thing beyond a reasonable doubt. Kenneth Brown was Amy's killer. Thank you."

Brunelle returned to his seat and allowed his heart to slow. He'd stayed right up on the razor's edge, despite Judge Grissom's warnings. But what choice did he have? The case was razor thin. He was reminded of a quote by Barry Goldwater when he ran for president in 1964: 'Moderation in the pursuit of justice is no virtue.'

Then again, Goldwater lost. Big.

"Ladies and gentlemen," Grissom interrupted his thoughts, "please give your attention now to Ms. Edwards who will deliver the opening statement on behalf of the defendant."

CHAPTER 32

Edwards stood up and nodded to the judge. "Thank you, Your Honor." She stepped around the defense table, laying a reassuring hand on her client's shoulder on her way, and stepped into the attorney well. She set a large binder on the bar next to her and opened it to whatever page she wanted showing, then looked up the judge again, "May it please the court," she began ceremonially, turning to each addressed party in turn, "counsel, members of the jury. My name is Jessica Edwards, and I'm pleased to deliver the opening statement on behalf of my client, Mr. Kenneth Brown."

She was more formal than Brunelle, an attribute that would tend to benefit her client. There was an unspoken, underlying dynamic in a criminal prosecution: the prosecutor and judge were working to enforce the rules of the body politic and the defendant was a radical, unrepentant agent of chaos, bent on destroying the peace and prosperity of the good people of the world—a threat to be extinguished lest it consume us all. And Edwards represented him. She acted as a stand-in in the jury's eyes—since it was highly unlikely they would ever hear a word uttered from his lips.

'Better to let the world think you a respectable businessman than to open your mouth and confirm the fact that you're a low-life street pimp.' Or something like that.

So the more formal Edwards was, and the more she could show the jury she was part of the system, too, the better it would be for her client. It was all subliminal, of course, but very real.

"Amy Corrigan may be dead," Edwards began. "Or then again, maybe she's not. She might have run off to another city or state, or even another country. Or maybe she didn't. She might be buried deep in the ground somewhere or she might be way up in a penthouse starting a new life, looking down and wondering if anyone from Seattle even noticed she left."

Edwards shrugged to the jury. "We don't know. No one knows. Because Amy Corrigan just disappeared. She didn't leave behind any clue as to where she was going. But, then again, that happens a lot when people run away. The whole point of running away is so people can't find you. It would defeat the purpose if you told them where you were going."

She took two steps to her right, head lowered in apparent thought, then stopped again and looked back to the jury. "But not leaving anything behind—that's very strange when a person is murdered. When a person is murdered they always leave something behind: their body."

Touché, thought Brunelle. But he didn't let the thought appear on his face. He was bent over his notepad, taking notes with an air of calm confidence—at least that was the appearance he was going for.

Edwards continued. "When someone dies, they leave their body behind. It doesn't matter how they died. Unless the body is completely vaporized in some sort of accident, there's a body left behind to confirm the person is dead. When an old man passes away in his sleep, his family finds his body in the bed. When someone dies in a car crash, paramedics pull the body from the wreckage. And when someone is murdered... Well, it's pretty hard to get rid of a body and erase any trace of evidence at the crime scene. In fact, the body usually tells us exactly how the person died—strangulation, stab wounds, gunshot—and the crime scene often tells us who did it. The ex-wife's living room covered in the victim's blood? Pretty likely she'll be suspect number one."

Edwards nodded to herself and retraced those two steps back to her original standing position. "But in this case, there's no sign of Amy Corrigan's body. It wasn't found in a bed, or a car, or Mr. Brown's living room."

Brunelle's eyebrow raised. Edwards had very subtly, and very deftly suggested that Brown and Corrigan were exes. He knew it was intentional. He was less sure if it helped her case. On the one hand, it suggested he cared for her. On the other hand, domestic violence murders were hardly unheard of. It's hard to get murderously angry at a simple co-worker.

"In this case," Edwards continued, "Amy Corrigan disappeared without a trace. Something far more common in runaway cases than murder cases. In fact, it's just the opposite of what you'd expect in a murder case."

Brunelle lowered his pen and frowned. The frown came for three reasons. One, Edwards was making a good point and doing so rather effectively. Two, she *was* being argumentative though—something lawyers aren't supposed to do in opening statement. Three, he could therefore object, even though he really didn't like objecting. Hence the frown; it was one of indecision. Because, despite his distaste for playing the objecting obstructionist, reason two meant reason three would be sustained, thereby stopping reason one.

His indecision was overcome by Edwards' next comments. "So, I'm going to challenge you, ladies and gentlemen. I'm going to challenge you not to be swayed by passion and innuendo, but rather to base your decision on the evidence—or rather the lack of it. A missing body—"

"Objection," Brunelle said calmly—almost quietly—as he stood up. "Argumentative."

The other reason Brunelle went ahead and objected was because Edwards had interrupted his opening statement, twice. It wasn't just to get her back—not *just* that—but also because he didn't want the jury left with the impression that he was willing to do something inappropriate but Edwards was the legal profession's Mother Teresa.

Grissom leaned forward, glanced at Brunelle almost as if to confirm he really had stood up and made an objection, then turned to Edwards. "It does seem argumentative, counsel. Opening statement is supposed to be limited to what you believe the evidence will show. The facts, as it were. Not arguments as to the legal significance of those facts. And not challenges to the jury to find a particular way."

Edwards, who had turned to face the judge, didn't argue, but simply offered a tight smile and a curt nod. "Yes, Your Honor. Thank you, Your Honor."

She turned back to the jurors. "The judge is correct. Opening statement is supposed to be what we think the evidence will show. But, ladies and gentlemen, that's the whole problem. The evidence is going to show nothing. It's not going to show Amy Corrigan was murdered. It's not even going to show that she's dead. It's going to show that she disappeared and hasn't been heard from since, and there are any number of explanations for that which don't involve her death, let alone that my client killed her." Her voice was rising in volume and accelerating in cadence. Professionalism was giving way to passion—not necessarily a bad thing in trial. Jurors want to see you believe in your cause. "The evidence," Edwards waved a hand at Brunelle even as she kept her eyes on the jurors, "is going to show that there *is* no evidence. Instead, the prosecution is going to put on a series of witnesses who have no idea where Amy Corrigan is in the hopes of creating a cloud of guilt to disguise the undeniable fact that Kenneth Brown is absolutely not guilty of the charge of murder. Thank you."

Edwards snatched up her binder—which she never looked at—and hurried back to her seat. Brunelle frowned slightly to himself. That still sounded pretty argumentative. Unfortunately, it also sounded pretty accurate.

"Mr. Brunelle," Judge Grissom peered down at him, "the state may call its first witness."

Brunelle stood up and nodded to the judge. "The state calls Mary Corrigan."

CHAPTER 33

Mary Corrigan was Amy's mother. The only better person to start with would have been Lydia. But generally, toddlers weren't competent to testify. So Brunelle would have to forgo the theater of a two-year-old telling the jury, 'I miss my mommy,' and go instead to the mommy's mommy.

Mary walked into the courtroom rather uneasily and looked around at the proceedings. Lawyers and jurors, judges and defendants, armed guards and interested spectators. It was a lot. Her face showed her anxiety. The downside of starting with Mary was that civilian witnesses weren't usually very good at testifying. Cops and crime lab scientists knew the drill: sit naturally, answer just the question that was asked, turn to the jury to speak. They were used to it. But civilians could get overwhelmed. Especially family. Especially mom.

But that was also part of the appeal for Brunelle. Let mom break down on the stand. Let the jury see how devastated she is at the loss of her daughter. Let Edwards attack her and have the jury hate her client for it. Mary didn't have any information about how Amy died—hell, Brunelle didn't even have that—so she could hardly say anything to damage his case. She was there to introduce the jury to Amy, and to convince them Amy would never run away. Not from little Lydia.

Mary walked nervously through the gauntlet of spectators and approached the witness stand. She clutched her purse in her left hand as she raised her right and the judge swore her in. Then she sat down and Brunelle started his examination.

"Please state your name for the record," he began.

"Mary Corrigan," she answered. She glimpsed quickly around the room, then returned her gaze to Brunelle.

Ordinarily, Brunelle preferred a witness to give their answers to the jury, but he'd done this long enough to know the nervous witnesses needed to focus in on the questioner and half-forget anyone was watching. He took a step closer to her to affirm their connection.

"Thank you for coming today, Ms. Corrigan." The only pleasantry he had time for. They couldn't pretend it was a social visit. "Did you know Amy Corrigan?"

Mary nodded. "Yes," was all she managed to say.

Brunelle nodded back, half acknowledgment of how difficult this was going to be for her, half encouragement to do it anyway. "And who was Amy Corrigan?"

Mary took a moment to respond. Her lip quivered. "My daughter," she croaked over the lump in her throat.

Brunelle nodded again, then stepped back to his table. He picked up a photograph and showed it briefly to Edwards. Edwards nodded and waved him forward. Brunelle approached the witness stand and handed the photograph to Mary.

"Do you recognize the person in this photograph?" he asked.

Of course she did. He knew that; everyone in the courtroom

knew that. But the evidence rules required he lay foundation before he could show the picture to the jury. And, really, that was one of the two main reasons for calling Mary Corrigan. To show the jury that Amy Corrigan was a real, honest to goodness, living and breathing person; and to tell them what she'd left behind.

Mary looked at the photograph. Her eyes welled and she nodded. She closed her eyes and a tear rolled down her cheek, "Yes," she sniffled. "That's Amy."

Brunelle reached out and took the photograph back. "Your Honor, the state moves to admit exhibit number one."

"No objection," Edwards said.

"Exhibit one is admitted," the judge ordered.

There was a box of tissues on the witness stand. Brunelle slid it to Mary, then stepped over to the projector between the lawyers' tables and placed the photograph on it. A moment later, Amy's smiling face was blown up four-feet tall on the screen across from the jurors.

"That's Amy?" Brunelle confirmed with Mary.

Mary nodded again, a tissue pressed to her nose. "Yes. That's my Amy."

Perfect, Brunelle thought. '*My* Amy.' Couldn't have been a better response. He was half way there.

The photo was what was commonly referred to as an 'in life' photo. It was meant to contrast the 'in death' photographs: bloody at the crime scene, scrubbed and pale on the medical examiner's slab. In the normal murder case, the in-life reminded the jury that the corpse used to be a real person. But this wasn't the normal case. The smiling face of Amy Corrigan wouldn't just remind the jury that Amy Corrigan used to be alive—without the bloody crime scene and creepy autopsy photos, there was a danger it would leave them with the impression that she might still be alive. Best to rebut that idea right away.

"When was the last time you saw Amy?" Brunelle asked. He left the photo up on the screen. He was going to leave it up for the next line of questioning, until he replaced it with another photo to finish his examination—one he hoped Edwards would forget was up when she did her cross.

Mary's brow furrowed in thought for a moment. She choked back a sob. "About six months ago."

Seven months and two weeks, Brunelle knew. At least that's how long it had been since Chen had called him down to watch Linda's interview. So probably a week or two more since the last time Amy had stopped by to see her mom and dad, and daughter. That was the next line of questioning. But there was a trap along the way.

“How often did you see Amy before that?”

Mary thought for a moment or two, then answered, “Every week, mostly. Sometimes more often, but not usually. She didn’t usually go more than a couple weeks before she’d come around again.”

The trap was that Mary couldn’t tell the jury what Amy was doing in between those visits, namely hooking for Kenny Brown. Brunelle had worried that Mary would be upset that the judge was keeping out important evidence about her daughter’s disappearance and murder. That was how it usually went: Brunelle would tell the witness that the judge had suppressed some piece of evidence that the witness wanted to talk about. An argument would ensue, except that Brunelle had no authority to change the ruling. One cop had even threatened not to swear ‘to tell the truth, the whole truth, and nothing but the truth’ since the judge had eliminated part of ‘the whole truth.’

But Mary was more than happy not to talk about her

daughter's occupation. She said she didn't want her dead daughter called a whore in public. And Brunelle figured Mary probably didn't want her own parenting questioned either. So they had an easy agreement not to mention it. Brunelle just had to hope she'd remember it while under the stress and distraction of testifying.

The trick was to stay as far away from the topic as possible. He could have asked a professional witness something like, 'What was she doing during that time?' and they would know not to mention anything about pimps and prostitutes. He couldn't quite trust Mary, so he just avoided the subject entirely and got to the main point: "When Amy came around, who was she coming to visit?"

Mary nodded. "Me and Howard, her dad. But really, it was to visit Lydia."

Brunelle allowed himself a quick glance out of the corner of his eye at the jury. The few faces he could see from that angle seemed interested. *Good,* he thought. As long as they were really paying attention, he could extract the information quickly, not risk further testimony from a distraught civilian, and sit down.

"Who's Lydia?"

Mary sniffled and finally turned to the jury; she was going to tell them directly. *Awesome,* Brunelle thought as the mother of the victim looked at the good people of the world who'd come to judge her daughter's killer and told them, "Lydia is Amy's daughter."

Brunelle let out a sigh of relief. He just needed to wrap up the details and see if Edwards dared to attack poor, sweet Mary Corrigan.

He took another photograph from his counsel table and showed it to Edwards. Edwards again nodded, barely looking at it, and Brunelle walked it over to Mary. "Do you recognize the person depicted in this photograph?"

Mary nodded. "Yep. That's Lydia."

"How old is she in that photo?" Brunelle asked.

"That was at her birthday party last fall," Mary answered. "She turned two. So she's more like two-and-a-half now."

Brunelle decided to stick the sympathy dagger a bit deeper into the jury's hearts. "Was Amy there for her birthday party?"

But Mary squirmed in her seat. Not what Brunelle wanted. He felt a flush race up the back of his neck as he remembered that old lawyer's saying: 'Never ask a question you don't know the answer to.'

"Uh, no," Mary answered reluctantly. "She couldn't make it. Uh, because, uh…"

Brunelle had to jump in. Mary knew not to mention the prostitution, but that didn't mean she knew what to say in its place.

"But she usually visited Lydia when she could?" he interrupted.

"Oh, yes, yes." She again turned to the jury, this time to try to convince them that Amy really was a good mother to Lydia. "She even came by that day, but it was late. She missed the party. But she kissed Lydia good night. She was so sad that she missed the party. She cried. It was so hard. She, just… It was really hard for her. It was hard for all of us. But she loved that little girl. She loved her more than anything in the world."

Brunelle was grateful for that last bit of testimony. But that still hadn't gone quite as well as he'd hoped. He suddenly remembered the photograph he'd handed Mary and looked up to the judge. "The state moves to admit exhibit two."

Again Edwards was ready. "No objection."

"Exhibit two is admitted," Grissom declared.

Brunelle walked over to the projector and replaced Amy's photo with Lydia's. It was definitely a birthday party. Lydia was definitely the birthday girl—and she definitely looked neglected. Her hair was tangled, her shirt dirty. But she was smiling for the camera. Even though her mommy missed her birthday party.

"How often did Amy visit Lydia, did you say?" Brunelle asked from over by the projector.

"Maybe every week or so," Mary repeated.

Brunelle nodded. "Did she ever miss a visit?"

Mary shrugged. "I mean, sure. Sometimes. But if she did, we'd always see her the next weekend. Well, usually."

Brunelle breathed in through his nose. The examination wasn't going quite as well as he'd wanted. Lydia was supposed to be the reason why the jury could be sure Amy was dead, not just missing. But Mary was chipping away at that theory with every 'sometimes' and 'usually,' Time to finish up. He walked back to his usual spot between his table and the jury box.

"So six months ago," he started, "when Amy didn't come to visit Lydia on schedule, it didn't concern you at first, right?"

An incredibly leading question, Brunelle knew, but Edwards didn't bother objecting.

"Um, right," Mary admitted. "We just figured we'd see her the next weekend."

"And did you?" Brunelle asked.

Mary cocked her head at him. "Did I what?"

Brunelle kept his poker face, but just barely. Sometimes, he really hated civilian witnesses. "Did you see Amy the next weekend?"

"Oh," Mary replied. "No. No, we didn't."

"How about the next weekend?" Brunelle followed up.

"No, no," Mary answered. "Like I said, we never saw her again. She just stopped coming. We never heard from her again. That's how we knew something terrible had happened."

Finally Edwards stood up. "Objection, Your Honor. The witness is speculating."

Brunelle frowned. Edwards was right. Witnesses couldn't speculate. He looked up to the judge, but no argument came to him. Grissom saw it in his eyes. "Objection sustained, Mr. Brunelle. The witness can report her contact with her daughter, but she can't speculate as to why it ended."

Brunelle nodded. It didn't matter. The jury understood. And he'd be allowed to argue it in closing argument. "Thank you, Your Honor."

He turned back to Mary Corrigan and went through his mental checklist for her examination: mother, in-life photo, Lydia, photo of Lydia, hadn't seen Amy for six months. Yep, that was everything.

"No further questions," he announced and returned to his seat. It was Edwards' turn.

She stood up and double checked her notes. Then she stepped over to the projector and turned it off. Lydia's smiling face disappeared from the screen.

"Assuming Amy visited you every two or three weeks," Edwards said, "you only saw her maybe twenty times a year, correct?"

Mary's face contorted a bit as she tried to do the math. "Uh, maybe. I don't know. I guess so. I mean, it seemed like more than that."

Edwards nodded at the answer and moved to the next question. "And she sometimes missed important occasions like her daughter's birthday, correct?"

"She only missed the party," Mary protested. "She made it before her birthday ended."

"She wasn't always reliable, was she, Mrs. Corrigan?"

Edwards pressed.

Mary narrowed her eyes. "There were reasons," she snarled.

Oh, shit, Brunelle thought. If Mary got too angry at Edwards, she might go ahead and mention the prostitution, just to spite her. It was one thing to do what the prosecutor told you when he was standing in front of you. It was another to let a defense attorney mischaracterize your daughter.

But Edwards stepped back from the precipice. "I know, Mrs. Corrigan," she assured, almost motherly. "I know."

She paused long enough for Mary, and the jury, to realize she wasn't such a bitch after all. "And I know you have your opinion about what happened to Amy to cause her not to come visiting for over six months but, really, based on just the facts and just on what you yourself personally know—you don't actually know what happened to Amy, do you?"

Mary shifted her weight again. The line between what a person believes and what a person knows can be blurry. Especially when that person is a mother.

"I know what happened to my daughter," Mary insisted.

Edwards frowned for a moment. Then she crossed her arms and tried a different approach, "If Amy came home tonight, you'd be pretty surprised, wouldn't you?"

Mary was quick to nod emphatically. Her tears had dried. Her expression was clearly one of contempt for the woman defending her daughter's killer. "Damn right I would."

"But it's not impossible, is it, Mrs. Corrigan?" Edwards asked.

Mary hesitated.

"Based on what you actually know yourself," Edwards pressed, "it's not impossible, is it?"

Mary opened her mouth to answer, but the reply got caught

in her throat.

Edwards' expression softened sympathetically. "There's still a part of your heart that hopes it's not impossible, isn't that right, Mrs. Corrigan?"

Mary looked Edwards in the eyes, then dropped her gaze to the floor. "Yes," she admitted, choking back another sob. "I hope it's not impossible."

Edwards nodded. "No further questions."

Brunelle looked at the woman on the witness stand. She was in no shape for further questioning. And he wasn't sure how to rehabilitate her anyway. Edwards was right. But the last shred of hope of a distraught mother didn't mean Amy Corrigan was alive. It just meant Mary was a mother. And that was better left to closing argument.

"Any redirect examination, Mr. Brunelle?" Judge Grissom asked.

Brunelle stood. "No, Your Honor. This witness may be excused."

Mary looked up again, visibly relieved but also shaken. She probably had no idea how her testimony had helped or hurt the case—Brunelle himself wasn't even sure at that point. But talking about your probably-dead daughter, whose death had come at the hands of drug addiction and a brutal pimp, would drain anyone. She clutched her purse in both hands and made her way out to the hallway where Brunelle knew Howard Corrigan was waiting for her.

Then Brunelle returned his thoughts to the job at hand: laying out his case-in-chief. Now that the emotional aspect had been put to the jury, it was time to talk about the investigation.

"The state calls Larry Chen to the stand."

CHAPTER 34

Chen strode confidently into the courtroom. His large frame pushed through the doors and made its way directly to the witness stand. He knew the drill. The judge did too. In a matter of moments Chen was sworn in, seated, and ready for Brunelle's first question.

"Please state your name for the record," Brunelle started. Not really a question, but pretty much the best way to start a direct exam.

"Larry Chen."

"How are you employed, sir?" Brunelle moved to the usual second question, at least for cops and other professionals.

"I'm a detective with the Seattle Police Department." Chen was delivering all of his answers to the jury, just like they taught all the cops at the academy. That was good; it brought the jurors into the action, but Brunelle knew they'd lose interest fast if Chen didn't provide some good information after the introductions.

Mary Corrigan had been a good first witness. Emotional, and it got those photos up on the screen. It explained that Amy hadn't been seen for quite some time. But it didn't explain why. That would be Chen's job.

"What kind of cases do you investigate, detective?"

"Homicides, mostly," was his response. "And other major crimes. Rapes, robberies, serious assaults."

"Do you investigate missing person cases?" Brunelle asked, as if he didn't already know the answer.

Chen shook his head. "No. I haven't done a missing person case for years. That's more junior detective stuff. Or even senior patrol officers."

Brunelle nodded. "So you don't handle missing person cases?"

Chen shook his head again. "No, sir, I don't."

"Did you handle the Amy Corrigan case?"

Chen looked at the jury. "Yes, sir, I did.

Brunelle smiled inside. He enjoyed doing the direct exam song-and-dance with Chen. They were good at it. He had a vague recollection that they'd had a falling out recently, but his mind was too busy with the task at hand to bother remembering why. They were good, and they were together again. Nothing else mattered right then.

"Please explain to the jury," Brunelle inclined his head toward the jury box, "how a homicide detective came to be involved in the Amy Corrigan case."

Chen nodded to Brunelle, then turned again to the jurors. "I was working on a stabbing that happened down on East Marginal Way, down by the First Avenue Bridge. A couple of homeless guys. One of them said the wrong thing and the other guy had a knife. The guy with the knife took off and we were left with just a dead guy on the street. No witnesses, no leads, no nothing."

Brunelle nodded along with the story, but didn't interrupt his witness.

"We started asking around if anyone had seen anything,"

Chen continued. "Usual stuff. Local businesses, stuff like that. Everyone we talked to insisted they hadn't seen anything, but they would usually give us the name of someone else to talk to who maybe did see something. It was going nowhere, but then we got the name of Linda Prescott."

Brunelle frowned slightly at the name. He'd forgotten about her a little bit, since he couldn't prosecute anyone for her death. Then he remembered he'd solicited her for sex—fake sex, but still. It was a weird conflux of emotions, so he shook himself out of it and returned his attention to Chen.

"Did Linda have information about that murder?" Brunelle asked, knowing the answer.

"No." Chen shook his head. "But she had information about another murder."

"Whose murder?" Brunelle followed up.

An earnest look to the jury from Chen. "Amy Corrigan's."

Brunelle nodded again. His way of mentally checking off the bullet points of his direct examination.

"What did Linda tell you about Amy Corrigan's murder?"

"Objection." Edwards stood up, calmly enough, but her voice was still forceful. "The question calls for hearsay."

Grissom turned from Edwards' objection to Brunelle's reply. "Response?"

Brunelle frowned. It was hearsay—sort of. Hearsay was anything a witness said outside of a courtroom that a different witness told the jury about. 'I didn't see Jimmy steal the apple, but Cindy told me she saw it." Well then, Cindy needed to come in and tell the jury what she saw—and get cross-examined by Jimmy's defense attorney. But that was just it, Linda wouldn't be coming in to testify—she was dead. And Edwards knew that. Hence the objection.

"It has a non-hearsay use, Your Honor," Brunelle replied. There were two ways to get hearsay admitted: first, it might fit one of the so-called 'hearsay exceptions' where the circumstances suggest the speaker probably wasn't lying. Descriptions to a 911 operator while a crime is occurring, statements to a doctor for medical treatment, a dying declaration to a loved one just before you pass away. But none of those really fit. Linda died, but not right then, so that wasn't going to do it.

The second way to get hearsay admitted was if it was being admitted for a non-hearsay use, that is, for some reason other than a desire for the jury to believe what the speaker was saying. If it's not about what the speaker said, then it doesn't matter if the jury hears it.

"What's the non-hearsay use?" Grissom asked dubiously.

"It goes to what the detective learned and what steps he took afterward," Brunelle explained. "It goes to the detective's state of mind and explains why he did what he did next."

Grissom frowned, obviously unimpressed by this excuse to admit hearsay without calling it that. She turned back to Edwards. "Any response to that, Ms. Edwards?"

Edwards crossed her arms. "That's just a flimsy excuse, Your Honor. That's what lawyers always say when they want to admit hearsay but there's no exception for it. The detective can testify to what steps he took, if any, without having to relate Linda Prescott's untested assertions to jury."

Grissom nodded. "I'm going to sustain the objection. You can elicit what steps the detective took after speaking with Ms. Prescott, but you can't elicit what Ms. Prescott told him."

Brunelle sighed, but he wasn't surprised by the ruling. That's why it was so frustrating that Linda had died. Well, that, and he didn't want anyone to die before their time. But right then, it was mostly about how her death was damaging his case-in-chief. Luckily, it wasn't his first rodeo. He knew how to tell the jury what Linda said without actually telling the jury what she said.

"Let's do it this way," Brunelle directed Chen. "Did you speak with Linda Prescott?"

Chen nodded. "Yes."

"Did she provide you with information?"

Another nod. "Yes."

"And based on that information, what steps did you take?"

Chen looked to the jury. "I opened a homicide investigation."

"What was the name of the victim in that investigation?"

"Amy Corrigan."

And the big one: "Did you have a suspect?"

"Yes, I did."

"Who was the suspect?"

Chen turned again to the jurors. "The defendant, Kenneth Brown."

Brunelle smiled inside. That may actually have been better than relating exactly what Linda said. Now the jury knew Linda told Chen that Brown killed Amy. And they knew Edwards didn't want them to hear that.

That was the main thing. But there was a bit more.

"I'd like to go back," Brunelle said, "to that other murder you mentioned. The man who was found stabbed to death on East Marginal Way. How did you say that investigation began?"

"We got a 911 call about a dead body on the sidewalk," Chen answered. "Patrol was dispatched and, sure enough, there was a dead guy on the street. So they called for a homicide detective and I went out to the scene."

"And do most of your cases start that way?" Brunelle asked.

"By someone finding a body?"

Chen nodded. "Most of them. Sometimes the victim is still alive and dies at the hospital, but yeah, we get a lot of them where the victim is already dead on the scene."

"Do cases ever start without a body being found?"

Chen thought for a moment—mostly theatrics for the jury. He knew the question was coming. But no reason not to look like his answer was well considered. "Sometimes. It's rare, but it does happen."

"How do those usually start?" Brunelle asked.

"Usually by a family member reporting the person missing," Chen told the jurors.

"So it starts as a missing persons case?" Brunelle suggested.

But Chen shook his head. "Not necessarily. It depends. If the person went missing and there's blood all over the ex-boyfriend's truck, well, then, it probably starts as a homicide. If it's just, 'We haven't seen Jane since last Tuesday,' then maybe it starts as a missing person case. It just depends on the facts."

"What about this case?" Brunelle asked. "What about Amy Corrigan's case?"

"No, that began as a homicide case," Chen assured.

"Based on what Linda Prescott told you?" Brunelle inquired.

"Yes," was the answer. "Absolutely."

Just one more area of inquiry for the detective, then Brunelle could end his examination. Detectives often testified more than once in a murder trial, and Brunelle already suspected he'd have to bring Chen back for a different issue if things went the way he feared later in his case. The goal for this session was to explain how the investigation started and emphasize that the experienced homicide detective took one look at it and knew right away it was a murder, not just somebody running away. And that he took steps to confirm it.

"Did you make any efforts to locate Amy Corrigan?" Brunelle asked him.

"Of course," Chen replied. He gave his explanation to the jurors. "It's pretty much impossible to disappear any more. Back in the old days, you could just move to a new city, adopt a new name, and start your life over. Now, that's pretty much impossible. We can track people wherever they go, by credit card usage, rental applications, whatever. Every time anybody does anything, there's an electronic record of it. And all of those records can be sorted through and compiled by individual. I checked every local, state, and federal database for any sign of Amy Corrigan. I ran her social security number, driver's license number, and fingerprints through everything at my disposal. There has been absolutely no sign of Amy Corrigan since she disappeared."

Brunelle was almost done. One more question, and since he knew Chen, he knew the answer.

"When was the last time you checked?"

"This morning," Chen answered, "just before I came to the courthouse."

Brunelle nodded, satisfied with his examination of the detective. "No further questions."

As Brunelle sat down, Edwards stood up and approached the witness stand. She had her binder again and set it on the bar, open to some page about a third of the way through the several hundred pages contained within.

"You've never found a body, correct?"

Chen nodded. "That is correct."

"So you can't say with absolute certainty that Amy Corrigan is dead, can you?"

Chen shrugged slightly. "Not with absolute certainty. No,

ma'am."

Chen was being professional and honest, admitting the weaknesses in the case rather than exacerbating them but looking defensive.

"It's possible she's still alive, isn't it?" Edwards pressed.

This time Chen chewed his cheek for a moment. "No, ma'am. I don't think so."

Edwards frowned. Brunelle stopped himself from smiling.

"Why is that?" Edwards had to follow up. One of the rules of cross examination was never to ask open-ended questions like 'Why?' and 'How?' Instead, make statements and force the witness to agree. Edwards was good enough to do that. But sometimes, to also avoid looking defensive, you have to ask the follow up question the jury wants the answer to.

"Well, ma'am," Chen looked again to the jury to explain, "as I said before, it's pretty much impossible to live any more without leaving some sort of trace behind. If Amy Corrigan were alive, I'd know it."

Edwards paused, debating her next question.

"Okay, I'm not sure I agree with you," she started. "But let's assume for a moment that she's dead and not just trying to avoid detection by friends or family or law enforcement. You don't have any idea how she died, do you?"

Chen paused for a moment. Then he inclined his head at Edwards. "I always have ideas. I'm a detective."

Chen was doing a good job parrying with Edwards. Brunelle stopped taking notes so he could just pay attention, enjoy the show.

"I'm sure you do," Edwards replied with a saccharine grin. "But unlike the man on East Marginal Way, you can't say how she died, can you? You can't say she was stabbed, or shot, or strangled, or whatever, can you?"

Chen had to admit that. "No, ma'am. I can't tell you the exact manner of death."

"And similarly," Edwards asserted, "however she died, you don't know who was there when it happened, do you?"

Chen offered a slight smile. "Again, Ms. Edwards. I have my ideas." Then he looked over at Kenny Brown.

Edwards bristled. "Let's not speculate, detective. You don't know how Amy Corrigan died, you don't know who was with her when she died, and, in fact, you don't even know whether she's dead, isn't that all true, detective?"

"Objection." Brunelle finally stood up, but mostly to join in Chen's game. "Compound question."

Edwards huffed. Grissom sustained the procedural objection. Brunelle sat down again, pleased with himself.

"You don't actually know how Amy Corrigan died, do you, detective?" Edwards repeated.

"No, ma'am," Chen conceded. Part of playing the game well was knowing when to stop.

"And you don't know who was with her when it happened, do you, detective?"

Chen thought for a moment. "I can't say for certain, no."

"And," Edwards wrapped up, "it's at least theoretically possible that Amy Corrigan is actually still alive and well as we sit here today, isn't that true, detective?"

Again Chen paused before replying. "I guess I would agree that it's theoretically possible, yes."

"Thank you, detective," Edwards said gruffly. Then she scooped up her binder and announced, "No further questions."

Grissom looked to Brunelle. "Any redirect examination?"

Brunelle stood up. "Yes, Your Honor."

He didn't have to prove the case beyond any doubt.

"It might be theoretically possible to believe Amy is still alive," Brunelle said, "but is it reasonable?"

Chen answered before Edwards could object again. "No, sir."

"No further questions," Brunelle said and he sat down again.

He just had to prove the case beyond any reasonable doubt.

Edwards had no recross, Chen was excused, and that completed the first day of trial. That was the good news. The bad news was Brunelle had to turn his attention to the star witness for the second day of trial. Chen may have stepped off the witness stand, but Brunelle wasn't done with him for the day.

After the jury filed into the jury room, and as the attorneys and court staff gathered up their things, Brunelle went out into the hallway to talk with his detective.

Chen was waiting for him. "Jillian Hammond," he said. "Right?"

Brunelle nodded. "Right. I need her first thing tomorrow. Can you secure her?"

"You mean, can I arrest her for prostitution, then bring her to the courtroom?" Chen translated. "Yeah, I can do that. She might be dressed in a tube top and stripper shoes, though."

"I don't care if she's dressed in Saran wrap," Brunelle replied. "I just need her on the stand. Grissom didn't let in Linda's statements. I need Jillian's."

Chen just stared back at Brunelle.

"What?" Brunelle asked.

Chen raised an eyebrow. "Saran wrap?"

Brunelle shook his head and laughed. "You know what I mean."

Chen laughed too. "I'm just busting your chops. You got it.

Jillian. Tomorrow morning. Saran wrap. Got it."

He patted Brunelle on the shoulder and walked away.

Brunelle lingered for a moment, glad no one had overheard their conversation.

But he was wrong.

CHAPTER 35

Brunelle suffered a long, restless night. His dreams tried to solve the dilemma his waking brain anticipated for the next day of trial. After far too little rest, he dragged himself out of bed, through the shower, and to the courtroom where Chen was waiting to confirm his fear.

"I couldn't find her."

Brunelle clenched a fist at his side. "Fuck."

"Yeah," Chen agreed. "I can't decide if I'm surprised or not."

Brunelle frowned at himself. "I scared her off. When I tried to serve her with the subpoena."

But Chen shook his head. "I don't think so. I talked to the other girls. They said she stuck around after that. She didn't disappear until last night. They were as surprised as me that she wasn't there."

Brunelle gazed at the ground in contemplation of what to do next. Then something occurred to him.

"Wait. How did they know what night I tried to serve the subpoena?"

Chen laughed. "I asked when the nervous guy in the suit got

beat up by their pimp."

Brunelle was dumbstruck. "How did you know I got beat up?"

Chen laughed again and pointed to Brunelle's still-healing cheek. "Pretty obvious."

Then Brunelle considered one more thing. "How did you know I was wearing a suit?"

Chen placed a friendly hand on Brunelle's shoulder. "Dave, you always wear a suit."

Brunelle frowned, but he could hardly argue.

"No worries, Dave. You wear a suit well."

Brunelle was speechless. He'd almost forgotten what they were talking about. Almost.

"So what do I do now?" he asked, more to himself than Chen. "I wanted to call Tina next."

"You mean Jillian?"

Brunelle just stared at Chen. "Right. Yeah. Jillian."

They stood in thought for a few moments. "So what are you going to do?" Chen finally asked.

Brunelle shrugged. "Can you keep looking for her?"

Chen nodded. "Of course. But I don't know how long it will take. What are you going to do in the meantime?"

Brunelle smiled and smoothed out that suit he wore so well. "Stall."

CHAPTER 36

One thing about a murder case was that there were usually a lot of witnesses. Civilians, first responders, crime scene techs, paramedics, ER doctors, patrol officers, detectives, medical examiners. That would normally have given Brunelle plenty of time to stall.

Normally.

But this case was different. The only civilians he had were Linda and Tina/Jillian, but Linda was dead and Jillian was M.I.A. There were no first responders or crime scene techs because there was no crime scene to respond to. There were no medical personnel because there was no body. The detective had already testified. So even with calling everyone even remotely related to the case, Brunelle was barely able to stretch things to the end of the week to buy Chen a weekend to find Jillian. But when Monday rolled around Chen didn't have Jillian, and Brunelle only had one witness left.

The medical examiner.

"The state calls Dr. Kat Anderson."

The judge and jurors had that fresh Monday morning look

to them. Attentive, not yet worn down by the week. Edwards looked sharp too. Even Kenny Brown seemed extra chipper, whispering with his attorney and generally looking like he felt good about his chances.

Brunelle, on the other hand, felt crappy. He hadn't slept well that weekend. He was worried about his case and doubtful Chen would find Jillian. Without her, he couldn't get Brown's confessions to the jury. If Chen tried to testify about it, Edwards would again cry hearsay, and Grissom would again sustain it. But the real reason he couldn't sleep was Kat.

He'd been able to throw himself into his work since they'd broken up.

'Broken up', he thought. Like it was mutual. He'd cheated on her and she'd found out. And the woman he'd cheated with, defense attorney Robyn Dunn, had enjoyed their tryst, then moved on almost before Kat was out the proverbial door.

So, single again despite feelings for two different women, work was his refuge. Typical, really. Almost pathetically predictable. But effective. Until he needed Kat again—professionally, that is.

He hadn't even bothered to call her to schedule her testimony. He had Nicole do it. Monday morning at 9:00 a.m. He knew she'd be on time. He could always count on her. Too bad the same hadn't been true about him.

He was feeling pretty low that morning, and figured Kat would also look down. He expected an awkward interaction, her expression sad, his guilty. So it was a surprise punch in the gut when she marched into the courtroom looking better than ever, a smile beaming on her remarkably pretty face.

She walked confidently to the witness stand and was sworn in by Judge Grissom. A moment later, everyone looked at Brunelle to start his direct examination. He hesitated, still distracted by how unexpectedly not-unhappy Kat looked. She wasn't radiating sunshine or anything. She just looked normal. Over it. Over him.

That stung more than he expected.

"Uh," he stammered, "Good morning."

"Good morning," Kat replied evenly.

"Please state your name for the record."

"Kat Anderson," she told the jurors.

"And how are you employed, ma'am?" He found solace in the familiar rhythm of the standard intro questions.

"I'm an assistant medical examiner with the King County Medical Examiner's Office."

"How long have you held that position?"

"Twelve years." Again, Kat looked at Brunelle when he asked the questions, then turned to the jury to deliver her answers.

"Do you hold any special degrees for your position?"

"I have a bachelor's degree in organic chemistry and a medical degree from the University of Washington," Kat explained. "I did my residency in forensic pathology at Harborview Medical Center, after which I was hired at the Medical Examiner's Office."

Brunelle nodded. Damn, she was pretty impressive.

"Okay, thank you," he said. Just a verbal tic to acknowledge the end of the intro. "Uh, did you have occasion to conduct an autopsy in this case?"

Kat raised an eyebrow at him. "Which case is that, counselor?"

Brunelle hesitated, then realized he was paying too much attention to his ex-girlfriend and not enough attention to the medical examiner. He'd spent days telling the jury there was no body and now he was asking a medical examiner about an autopsy.

"Uh, this is the Amy Corrigan case," he floundered. "But I

don't mean Amy Corrigan."

Fuck, he thought. *Get it together, man.*

Deep breath.

Reset.

"You never did an autopsy on anyone named Amy Corrigan, did you, doctor?"

Kat cocked her head. "Not recently," she answered. "I can't say I've never conducted an autopsy on someone with that name."

"Right," Brunelle said. "Right. I just meant recently. No Amy Corrigan recently, right?"

Kat nodded patiently. "Right."

"Because her body was never recovered?" Brunelle tried to clarify.

But Kat shrugged. "I don't know. I'm not a police officer."

Brunelle grimaced at himself. "Right."

Another deep breath. Another reset.

"Did you," he slowed his voice in an effort to slow his heartbeat, "recently perform an autopsy on a woman named Linda Prescott?"

Kat smiled slightly, like a mother whose child just figured out to stop touching the hot oven. "Yes."

The deep breaths were working. Brunelle was able to compartmentalize his screw up with Kat and focus on not screwing up the current case.

There was a reason Kat was there and it wasn't to reminisce. He needed to lay it out for the jury. Follow his mental bullet points and sit down.

"Are autopsies performed on all deaths in King County?" he asked.

"No," Kat explained. "Autopsies are only performed on cases where the cause of death is unclear, or where criminal agency is suspected."

Brunelle liked that answer. It suggested her death was criminal. "How did you come to conduct the autopsy on Ms. Prescott?"

"Seattle police were called out to a death at the Pacific Motel," Kat told the jurors. "It was late at night, almost midnight, I believe. I didn't go out to the scene; one of our technicians collected the body. It was stored until the next morning when I conducted the autopsy. One of several I did that day."

"And why was an autopsy necessary?" Brunelle wanted to push on that a little for the jurors.

"The cause of death was unclear," she explained. "She was found unresponsive in a motel room, with no apparent injuries." She thought for a moment. "Well, no apparent fresh injuries. There were older bruises at various stages of healing. And injection sites. But nothing to suggest a cause of death."

Brunelle nodded. He was liking how this was going. So far the jury had heard 'criminal agency', 'older bruises', and 'injection sites. They also knew, from Chen's testimony, that Linda knew Amy and told the cops she thought Brown had something to do with Amy's disappearance.

Her death, he reminded himself.

He and Kat had a good vibe going. Kind of like with Chen. It was nice. It felt comfortable. He almost forgot they'd broken up. But then he remembered again and felt a dump of acid in his stomach. He just needed to wrap up with Linda's autopsy and sit down.

"What was the result of your examination, doctor?" he asked.

"I conducted a full autopsy," she told the jurors. "Removing and inspecting each organ for any previously undetected abnormalities. I was looking for tumors or other pathologies. I found none. All of the organs were within normal size ranges and I found no signs of internal trauma. That left a drug overdose as the most likely cause of death, particularly in light of the injection sites I observed on her arms and feet."

"Feet?" Brunelle felt compelled to ask for some reason.

"Yes," Kat answered. "Severe drug addicts will often inject into their feet because it can be difficult after years of drug abuse to find a suitable vein in the arm. Also, it reduces the amount of injection site tracks left on the arm, which can be important if you want to diminish the appearance of being a drug addict."

Brunelle nodded. "Like, if you were in a profession where your personal appearance might influence how many clients you could get?"

That was close to edge, and Brunelle heard Edwards stir as if to object, but she let it go. Probably deciding it was better not to draw more attention to Brunelle's question by objecting to it.

"I suppose," Kat answered. "Or if you wanted to hide the tracks from friends or family."

Brunelle frowned slightly. A simple 'yes' would have been better.

"So how do you determine if someone died of a drug overdose?" he moved on.

"We have to send the blood out for toxicology analysis," Kat answered. "That takes a few weeks, so we hold off on a final determination until we get the results."

"And did you do that in this case?"

"I did," Kat confirmed.

"What were the results of the toxicology?"

Kat turned to the jury. "She had lethal levels of opiates in her system."

"Opiates?" Brunelle asked. He knew what that meant, but he

couldn't assume the jurors did.

"Heroin," Kat clarified. "She died of a heroin overdose."

Brunelle nodded one last time. He was done. It had gone well enough. And he enjoyed seeing Kat again, despite his earlier trepidation. He was glad for that too.

"No further questions."

Brunelle wondered what Edwards would do for cross. The issue wasn't really what Linda died from, but how she was related to Amy and Brown. Kat didn't have any information on that.

Edwards obviously knew that too. She stood up. "No questions, Your Honor."

She also knew Brunelle was out of witnesses.

"You may be excused, doctor," Judge Grissom told Kat. Kat stepped down from the witness stand and walked past Brunelle's table. He ventured a look at her, but she just walked past. Not like she was ignoring him. More like he wasn't worth ignoring. His heart sank again.

"Does the state have any more witnesses, Mr. Brunelle?"

Brunelle tore his thoughts from lost loves to lost witnesses. He didn't want to rest his case until he heard one more time from Chen. Once he rested, he couldn't re-open to call Jillian. He needed to stall just a bit more.

"I'd ask for a recess, Your Honor," he said. He didn't want to explain in front of the jury. He just needed to buy a little more time.

Grissom sighed but understood. It wasn't her first rodeo, either. She turned to the jurors. "Ladies and gentlemen, we're going to take a brief recess. I'm going to ask you to retire to the jury room while I discuss scheduling with the attorneys."

They had been sitting through the case long enough that there were now some audible, if still fairly good-natured, grumblings as the jurors stood up and walked into the jury room. Once the door closed, Grissom repeated her question to Brunelle.

"Do you have any more witnesses, Mr. Brunelle?"

Brunelle shrugged and threw a quick glance to the courtroom door. "I don't know, Your Honor. There is one more witness I'd like to call, but I'm not sure if I can find her."

Grissom frowned and looked at Edwards. "Are you ready to put on your witnesses?"

Edwards stood up. "Actually, Your Honor, Mr. Brunelle's case went a bit quicker than I'd expected. I don't mind giving him the rest of the morning to try to find his witness. We could come back after lunch. If we have her, great, we can take her testimony this afternoon. If not, he can rest his case. Either way, I'd ask the court's indulgence to allow me to start my case fresh tomorrow morning."

Grissom's frown deepened. "If Mr. Brunelle can't find his witness, that means we'll essentially just waste the rest of the court day."

Edwards nodded. "Yes, Your Honor. Unless you want to force Mr. Brunelle to rest right now. Then I might be ready to start after lunch."

Grissom turned back to Brunelle and raised an inquiring eyebrow. "I'd rather we go with Ms. Edwards' first suggestion, Your Honor. If I don't have my witness by one o'clock, I'll rest."

The judge folded her hands in front of her and thought for a few seconds. "Very well. We'll be at recess until one o'clock. Ms. Edwards, be prepared to put on your case first thing tomorrow, regardless of whether Mr. Brunelle can find his witness."

"Understood, Your Honor," Edwards replied. "I'll be ready."

Brunelle frowned. He knew she would be.

CHAPTER 37

Chen had no luck finding Jillian. She was in the wind. The only things he was able to confirm were that she'd been there the night before she disappeared, and she didn't tell anyone she was going anywhere. Brunelle was forced to rest his case without introducing Brown's confessions—his boasts, really—into evidence. That left his case perilously thin. He stayed late that night, staring blankly at his computer monitor long after most of the prosecutor's office staff had gone home for the night.

After watching Kat walk past him like he was just any other guy on the street, he didn't feel like going home to his empty apartment.

But he wasn't the only one at the office late that night.

"How goes the trial?"

Brunelle tore his thousand-mile-stare from his computer monitor to the man leaning on his doorframe. Matt Duncan. His boss.

Brunelle smiled. He liked Duncan. He wasn't surprised the boss was staying late at the office. Duncan cared about the job. He cared about justice. That just made it all the worse.

"Not great," Brunelle admitted. "The judge excluded any evidence of prostitution or pimping and my star witness went missing. I had to rest without calling her. So the case is a loose mess of inferences and innuendo. I hope the jury gets it."

Duncan nodded. "They usually do. I tried a lot of cases before I got the corner office. Now I spend my days sitting in budget meetings and attending public forums. But from what I remember, the jury usually got it right. Even when I lost, they got it right."

Brunelle nodded. "Thanks, Matt."

There was silence for a few moments as Brunelle considered saying the same thing to a young attorney one day. 'I lost the Amy Corrigan case, but, based on the evidence, the jury got it right.' The thought of it made him sick.

"You knew it was going to be a tough case, Dave," Duncan interrupted his thoughts.

Brunelle shrugged. "Yeah. I just thought it would go better, that's all."

"Is that why you charged it?" Duncan asked. "Because you thought it would go well."

Brunelle shook his head. "No. Like you said, I knew it would be hard."

"So why did you charge it?"

Brunelle thought for a moment. "Because it was the right thing to do. Because he murdered Amy Corrigan and he should be held responsible."

"Did you do your best?"

Brunelle shrugged again. "I don't know. I tried. It's just a difficult case. Totally circumstantial. I lost my star witness. Then I lost the next one. It's just…" but the thought trailed off.

Duncan stepped into Brunelle's office and sat down on a

guest chair. "Look, Dave, I'll tell you something my boss said to me back when I was still trying homicide cases. He said, 'Matt, this job can be damn hard some days. You have a plan for the day and within ten minutes of getting to the office, your plan is blown to hell. You spend all day putting out fires and reacting to what everyone else needs right that second and by the time five o'clock rolls around, you feel like you haven't done a damn thing.'"

Brunelle looked at Duncan. "That sounds familiar," he admitted.

"Yeah," Duncan said. "And then he told me, 'If you come in on time, and work your ass off all day, then you can go home proud you did your job.' Don't look back and ask, 'Did I do what I planned to do today?' Look back and ask, 'Did I work hard today? Did I do justice today?' And if you can honestly answer 'yes' to that question, then it doesn't matter what anyone else says or does. Even if it's a jury saying 'not guilty.'"

Brunelle leaned back in his chair. "Thanks, Matt."

Duncan stood up. "Sure thing. Now go home. Get some rest. Fight tomorrow's battle tomorrow."

Brunelle nodded. "Okay. Sounds good. Edwards calls her first witness tomorrow. I should get some rest so I'm sharp for cross."

"Who's her first witness?" Duncan asked.

But Brunelle shook his head. "I don't know. Probably the defendant. I don't think she has any other witnesses. I'd have more fun crossing him if I could ask him about being a pimp."

"And a murderer," Duncan added.

"Yeah, well, I get to ask about that," Brunelle said. "But I'm pretty sure he'll deny it."

"Yeah, probably," Duncan agreed with a laugh.

Then Brunelle pursed his lips. "I don't know, though. She

might not call him at all. He looks all clean and proper sitting there in his suit. I'm not sure how well he'd come across if he opened his mouth. He's still a street pimp. Edwards is smart. She might tell him to do that whole right-to-remain-silent thing."

Duncan nodded. "She's a good lawyer. I'm sure she'll make the right decision for her client. I guess you'll just have to show up tomorrow morning and see what she has in store for you. Maybe she'll surprise you."

"Great," Brunelle stood up too, and clicked off his computer. "I hate surprises."

CHAPTER 38

"The defense calls Jillian Hammond."

Brunelle nearly fell out of his chair. Then he bolted up from it, ready to object. Somehow. To something. But there was nothing to object to.

Jillian 'Tina' Hammond strutted through the courtroom doors and up to the witness stand. Unlike Kat, Jillian was happy to stare at Brunelle as she walked by. Brunelle wished she hadn't.

The judge swore Jillian in, and Edwards took her spot at the bar, binder open once again.

"Good morning, Ms. Hammond," Edwards began. "Could you go ahead and state your full name for the court reporter?"

"Of course," Jillian answered. She was dressed differently from the other times Brunelle had seen her. Rather than a short skirt and tight blouse, she had on jeans and a sweater, with simple boots and her hair in a ponytail. She looked like somebody's older sister. "Jillian Hammond."

"Tina," Brunelle muttered under his breath.

"Jillian," Edwards asked. "Do you know a woman named Amy Corrigan?"

"Yes, I do," Jillian answered.

"How do you know her?"

"We work in the same neighborhood," was the sanitized answer. "We run in to each other from time to time and talk about our days."

And nights, Brunelle thought less than generously. He was pissed.

"Do you know my client, Kenneth Brown?" Edwards asked next.

"I wouldn't say I know him exactly," Jillian answered. "But we've talked. He works in the same neighborhood, too."

Brunelle really hoped the jury understood what all that meant—that Kenny Brown was a pimp and Amy and Jillian were hookers—because he couldn't tell them. Damn Judge Grissom, he couldn't tell them.

"How about Linda Prescott?" Edwards continued.

Jillian affected a suddenly troubled expression. She nodded and cast her eyes downward. "Yeah, I knew Linda."

Brunelle managed not to roll his own eyes. Jillian was laying it on thick. His head was still spinning. Where had she been all this time that Chen was looking for her? Why was she testifying for Brown? And most frightening of all, what the hell was she going to say?

"When was the last time you saw Amy Corrigan?" Edwards asked.

Jillian took a moment to think. In case it wasn't clear, she put a finger to pursed lips and looked up at the ceiling. "I think it was probably about four months ago."

That was bullshit, Brunelle knew. Linda reported her missing three months before that.

"And did you two have a conversation?"

Jillian nodded. "Yes."

"What did you talk about?"

Jillian nodded again. "She told me she was going to go to California for a while. Just to get away from things. Lay low for a while. I guess she had a kid and things were getting real stressful and she just couldn't handle it all."

Brunelle couldn't believe his ears. He looked at the jury to see if they were believing theirs. He couldn't be sure, but they were all paying attention. Some of them had to be buying it. *Damn it.*

"Did she ever mention anything about Mr. Brown?"

Jillian frowned thoughtfully and shook her head. "No. Nothing about him. Just about needing to get away for a while."

"Have you seen her since?"

"Nope. I ain't seen her since she told me she was leaving for Cali. I figure she's still there, laying low and staying out of sight."

Brunelle felt his heart squeeze in his chest. Jillian had just killed his case. The jury would acquit in a matter of minutes.

"Thank you, Ms. Hammond," Edwards said, picking up her binder. "No further questions."

The judge peered down at Brunelle. "Any cross examination?"

Brunelle looked up at the judge, still shell-shocked. Of course there would be cross examination. There had to be. He couldn't just let that testimony stand unchallenged. But he had no idea what he was going to say. He stood up anyway. "Yes, Your Honor. Thank you."

He usually did direct exam from next to his table. It was far enough away to make sure the witnesses kept their voices up, and it was right next to the jury box so they could look at the jurors more naturally. On cross, he preferred to stand closer to the witness. Not so close as to seem overly aggressive, but close enough to show that he was challenging them, and also to keep them focused on arguing with him, not convincing the jury.

"Good morning, Ms. Hammond," Brunelle started. He wanted to call her 'Tina' just to be snarky, but the jury wouldn't get it—and he wouldn't be allowed to explain it.

"Good morning," she replied, her eyes narrowed and challenging. Brunelle didn't suppose someone who'd been mentally, physically, and sexually abused by scores of johns and pimps was going to be scared by a few questions from some guy in a suit. There was no point in trying to intimidate her. He'd just have to try to outsmart her.

"You say Amy told you she was going to California?" he started.

"Yep," Jillian answered confidently.

"Did she say where in California?" he asked.

Jillian hesitated. Brunelle knew she was trying to decide which was more believable, that she would or wouldn't specify a city. "Uh, I don't know. I don't think so. Just California."

"Oh, okay." Brunelle nodded. "And you said she mentioned having a kid?"

"Yeah, she had a kid," Jillian answered. "A daughter, I think."

"Did she talk a lot about her daughter?" Brunelle asked.

Jillian shrugged. "I dunno. Not a lot, but yeah, sometimes."

"Like when you were working?" Brunelle suggested.

Jillian's expression hardened just a bit. "No. Never when we were working."

Another hint to the jury as to what these women really did for a living.

"But often enough that you knew about the kid?" Brunelle confirmed.

"Yeah, I guess so," Jillian conceded.

"But then you say she was going to California—nowhere in particular, just California—to get away from her daughter that she liked to talk about except when you were working?"

"Uh…" Jillian seemed unsure how to respond.

"Objection." Edwards jumped in. "Compound question."

Before the judge could rule on the objection, Brunelle offered, "I'll rephrase." Then he looked back to the witness. "You testified that one of the things Amy was trying to get away from was her daughter, is that correct?"

Jillian nodded, raising her chin slightly in defiance. "Right."

"You don't have kids, do you?" Brunelle ventured. He hoped the moms on the jury wouldn't believe any woman would abandon their two-year-old daughter for four months or more. Brunelle knew from his job that all kinds of people did that, and worse, to their children. But jurors were usually good people who lived in suburbs and went to church—they expected everyone else was like them, or should be.

Jillian didn't like the question, but had to answer, "No. I ain't got no kids."

Okay, thought Brunelle. That was about all he could do to undermine her. It was time to challenge her directly.

"Isn't it true, Ms. Hammond, that you spoke with me and Detective Larry Chen of the Seattle Police Department several weeks ago about the disappearance and murder of Amy Corrigan?"

Brunelle had hoped the question would rattle Jillian, but she obviously had been expecting it. The jury, on the other hand, audibly stirred. *Good*, thought Brunelle, *listen up, folks*.

"I don't recall ever talking to any detective," Jillian answered. "But I'm pretty sure I've seen you before."

Brunelle raised an eyebrow. "The night we talked about

Amy?"

But Jillian shook her head. "No. The night Linda died. I'm pretty sure I saw your car in the parking lot just before the cops showed up."

That sent more than a stirring through the courtroom. There were several gasps, an 'a-ha', and at least one giggle. Not exactly the reaction he liked to hear when he was doing a cross. He felt his face flush at the accusation—mostly because it was true.

He knew the best course of action was to ignore it, since he couldn't deny it.

"You spoke with me and Detective Chen at Green Lake Park and we discussed the murder of Amy Corrigan, isn't that true?"

But Jillian shook her head. "No, I never talked to you or no detective about Amy."

"And you told us Amy just disappeared and never said anything about going to California or anywhere else, isn't that true?"

"I never talked to you," Jillian insisted.

"And isn't it true, Ms. Hammond, that you told us that the defendant, Kenneth Brown, told you— "

"Objection!" Edwards practically jumped over her counsel table. "Objection. The witness has repeatedly said she never spoke with Mr. Brunelle or any detective. Mr. Brunelle should not be allowed to start listing off things that my client allegedly said just to have the witness say she never said that. I can't unring that bell."

Judge Grissom's face wore an expression of concern. She looked at Brunelle. "Any response, Mr. Brunelle? Why should you be allowed to tell the jury what you claim Mr. Brown said if the witness is just going to deny it? Doesn't that make you into the witness?"

Brunelle was pissed. He was pissed at Jillian Hammond for

lying. He was pissed at Edwards for calling her as a witness. And he was pissed at Judge Grissom for excluding all the evidence about pimping and prostitution—the only thing that made the whole thing make any sense.

But he quelled the anger long enough to formulate a coherent and well-reasoned response. "I intend to recall Detective Chen to testify about this conversation. Under evidence rule six-thirteen, I can introduce evidence of prior inconsistent statements of a witness through a third party, but only after confronting the witness with the statements and giving them the opportunity to admit or deny them. If I don't challenge Ms. Hammond on these statements now, Ms. Edwards will object to Detective Chen testifying about them because I didn't follow the procedure required by the evidence rule."

The judge gave Brunelle an approving nod. She turned back to Edwards. "Counsel? I believe Mr. Brunelle is correct about the rule. And I expect you would object if he didn't follow proper procedure."

Edwards just stood there for a moment, weighing her options. "I will stipulate that Mr. Brunelle has confronted Ms. Hammond with the entire content of the conversation. If he wants to call Detective Chen to discuss it, I will not make an objection under evidence rule six-thirteen."

Brunelle saw that response for what it was: an effort to stop him right then, and to buy time to think of a different objection when Chen retook the witness stand.

"Your Honor," he began to complain, but the judge cut him off.

"I think that's a good solution," she ruled. "Mr. Brunelle, no more questions about exactly what the witness may or may not have told you and Detective Chen. Move on, if you have any more questions."

He did. And he was still pissed.

He looked Jillian directly in the eye. "Where were you last week?" he demanded.

She met his gaze. "Up, down, and all around."

Brunelle wasn't sure what that was supposed to mean. His expression showed it. She decided to rub his face in it a little bit.

"You should stick to being a lawyer," she teased. "You'll never make it as a spy."

Brunelle took a step back, not sure what to make of the comment, but suddenly very sure he was done giving her a chance to talk. "No further questions, Your Honor."

He walked back to his seat, even as Edwards quickly rose to confirm, "No redirect examination, Your Honor."

Jillian Hammond stepped down from the witness stand and past Brunelle's table. He didn't look up to see if she looked at him as she passed. His head was still swimming with what she'd said and how to counter it—if he even could.

He knew one thing: Jillian had made it possible for Edwards not to have to call her client to the stand. Defendants rarely helped themselves when they testified. Brunelle knew that; so did Edwards. Which is why as soon as Jillian exited the courtroom, Edwards stood up again and announced, "The defense rests."

That was it. One witness. Brunelle's witness. But Edwards' testimony. The final nail in the coffin of his case.

He barely noticed the judge ask him, "Any rebuttal witnesses, Mr. Brunelle?"

Everyone in the courtroom knew the answer to that. He'd just announced he was going to recall Chen. "Uh, yes, Your Honor. But I'm not ready to do that today. I, well, honestly, I didn't expect to have to put on a rebuttal case." Not a great thing to admit in front of the jury, but he was too drained not to be honest. "Could we adjourn until tomorrow morning?"

But Judge Grissom wasn't keen on wasting another day of trial on just one witness. Her expression showed her doubts about Brunelle's suggestion, so he jumped in with a bit of levity. "That will also give Ms. Edwards time to think of another way to exclude the detective's testimony."

A juror laughed, Edwards couldn't help but smile slightly and the judge gave in. "All right, Mr. Brunelle, we will adjourn until tom—"

"Wait!" Brunelle interrupted. He suddenly realized what had happened. And what he might be able to do about it. "Uh, could we reconvene at one o'clock again? I'll contact Detective Chen, and maybe we can do this this afternoon after all. Or maybe not. But, um, let's reconvene at one. All of us. Really. One o'clock."

Grissom's expression changed again from grudging acquiescence to budding curiosity. "Okay, Mr. Brunelle. One o'clock. You'll be ready to proceed?"

But Brunelle rubbed the back of his neck. "I'm not sure about that. But I'll be able to tell the court whether I'm able to proceed. And if not, I can guarantee I'll be ready to wrap this case up once and for all tomorrow morning."

He looked over at Kenny Brown as he finished his sentence and for the first time, the two men met eyes. Brown's gaze was fierce, but there was an aspect of fear in it. Like he didn't know what Brunelle was going to do, and was at least a little bit worried by it.

Good, Brunelle thought. He was going to need that.

CHAPTER 39

Brunelle called Chen. They discussed the plan. Chen arrived at the courtroom at five minutes before one. Edwards was already there. So was Brown. Chen fetched Brunelle from his counsel table, and they went into the same hallway they'd been in when Brunelle told Chen he needed Jillian Hammond to testify. Right outside the courtroom door.

"The case has gone to complete shit," Brunelle said. "Jillian told the jury Amy was in California and the judge wouldn't let me tell the jury what she really said. Once the jury gets the case tomorrow, they're going to acquit him. Then he can tell everyone in the world that he killed her and we can't recharge him because of double jeopardy."

"We may have gotten a break," Chen answered. "I think we may be able to find out where he dumped the body. When I couldn't find Jillian, I started asking questions. People are afraid of him, but they're afraid of the cops, too."

"If you find the body, we'll convict him for sure," Brunelle said. "It'll prove Amy isn't in California and I bet he left DNA or some other type of trace evidence on her body, even if it's decomposed."

"I know," Chen agreed. "But I don't know where it is quite yet. I still need to ask some questions. He must have had help burying the body. I've got a lead and I think they'll snitch, but I won't know until tonight."

"You have to find that body before tomorrow morning," Brunelle insisted. "If he can make it just one more day, it'll be too late."

"Okay," Chen answered. "But like I said, it's gonna take me all night to finish my investigation. And I can't get the body until the forensics team comes in tomorrow morning. The earliest I could start digging is seven a.m."

"That'll have to do," Brunelle said. "If you start digging at seven, you'll find it by nine easy. Call me as soon as you have it, and I'll buy you time to get from the grave to court. I can't wait to see the look on Edwards' face when you tell the jury you found Amy's body."

"I can't wait to see the look on Brown's face," Chen replied, "when the jury says 'guilty of murder in the first degree.'"

They finished their conversation and went their separate ways. Chen headed for the exit and Brunelle went back inside the courtroom. The bailiff was standing up and reaching for his gavel. Edwards was still seated at counsel table, reading from her binder. And Brown was just making his way back to the defense table as Judge Grissom emerged from her chambers and took the bench.

"Are you ready to proceed, Mr. Brunelle?" she asked.

"No, Your Honor," he was quick to reply. "My apologies, but I need to wait until tomorrow morning. If all goes as planned, I'll be ready to wrap this up by nine or nine-thirty."

Grissom frowned, but she hardly seemed surprised. "Very well, Mr. Brunelle. We will be adjourned until tomorrow morning at nine. But be prepared to call Detective Chen or move directly to closing arguments. Understood?"

"Understood," Brunelle replied. "Thank you, Your Honor."

Then court was adjourned and Brunelle could do nothing more but wait.

CHAPTER 40

Brunelle did need the body to save his case. That was true. Pretty much everything else he and Chen said in that hallway was complete bullshit. But someone had overhead their earlier conversation about Jillian testifying. It was a good bet that person would eavesdrop again if Chen was seen taking Brunelle out to the same hallway on the other side of the less than perfectly sealed courtroom doors. And it was an even better bet that that person was Kenny Brown.

Chen had no leads. No one was about to snitch out Brown. Brown likely had help disposing the body, but they had no idea who helped him. There was only one person they could say for sure knew where Amy's body was: Kenny Brown. So rather than spending the night interviewing snitches and assembling 'the forensics team' to dig up Amy's body, Chen set up surveillance on Brown and hoped he'd panic.

Brunelle was counting on the fact that the case had gone so well for Brown. The bastard could practically taste the acquittal. Murder One and he walks. He'd be untouchable on the street. A legend. The man who murders his girls and gets away with it. It was too tempting. He couldn't risk losing it. So maybe it wasn't panic as much as greed. And who could possibly be greedier than a man who forces women to have sex with strangers for money?

But Chen couldn't do the surveillance. Brown would recognize him. In fact, Chen had to do the opposite of surveillance; he had to pretend to be shaking down prostitutes and pimps for info. He had to pretend to do exactly what he told Brunelle in the hallway. Brown would check to make sure he was really doing it—to confirm it was true, to see how close Chen was getting, and to make sure the cops were occupied while he went to move the real body. So they needed someone else.

"Montero?" Chen called over his radio. He and Brunelle were still at the station. "Are the units in position?"

"Roger that, Larry," came her reply. "All units are ready. Ohlstrom and Watkins are stationed outside his motel room. Donnelly is north and Petersen is south. When he makes his move, we'll be on him. This'll be fun."

Chen smiled. "Nothing wrong with fun, but make sure you're not spotted. He knows your face, too."

"No worries, Larry," Montero replied. "I'm remote. I won't move in until the shovel hits the dirt."

Chen nodded. "Good." Then he looked to Brunelle. "I'm gonna head up to the Aurora Motel and start bothering hookers. I know that's more your thing, Dave, but I think maybe this time you should hang back and let the cops do the work."

Brunelle laughed. "Okay. Fine. I can probably go one night without talking to a hooker or getting beat up by a pimp. Keep me in the loop, though, okay? I want to know the minute we nail this fucker."

Chen smiled. "Sure thing, partner," he joked. "One of these days we'll have to get you a badge."

Brunelle shook his head. "That's okay. I've got a bar card."

Chen raised an eyebrow. "Oh, yeah. I bet my badge is thicker than your bar card."

Brunelle shook his head at the joke. "Save that shit for the ladies, detective."

Chen grinned. "Okay." He stood up. "Go grab yourself a cup of coffee or something. I'll call you when he's in custody. It could be a while."

Brunelle stood up to leave too, agreeing to the suggestion but wondering if there wasn't some way he could be a little closer to the action.

* * *

In the event, a Denny's in Seattle's Ballard neighborhood, a few miles west of the Aurora Motel, was Brunelle's compromise. He wasn't a cop, so he wasn't going to try to participate in a stake out. But he wanted to be close so when they caught him, he could go out to the scene and see Brown handcuffed as they finished unearthing Amy Corrigan's remains.

Seattle may be full of Starbuckses, but they close early and the coffee is stronger at Denny's anyway. He brought some work to do, but couldn't really focus, so spent most of the first hour playing games on his phone.

After another hour, it was nearly midnight, his battery was almost dead, and there was still no word from Chen or Montero. He was starting to get worried. What if this didn't work? What if Brown hadn't overheard their conversation in the hallway? What if Jillian just bolted on her own and what if Brown wasn't listening in on their second conversation either? What if Brown was at home getting a good night's rest while Brunelle and Chen were exhausting themselves before tomorrow's testimony?

He shook his head. Too much strong coffee. He was jittery, but still tired. Fatigued. It had been a long couple weeks. Long couple months. He didn't need any more coffee. He needed a walk. Some fresh air and streetlights to clear his head and calm his nerves.

Ballard was a mix of Seattle's old-fashioned maritime industry, with ocean-going fishing vessels cheek-to-jowl all along the waterfront, and the city's newly found tech culture, with gentrified retail/condo complexes being constructed atop the ruins of the neighborhood's old grain stores and two-bedroom craftsmen homes. The Denny's on Market Street was a hold-out of the older era, likely to soon be replaced by a development of boutiques and hipster apartments. On three sides, it held back the onslaught of gentrification. Brunelle opted to walk in the direction of the fourth side: south, toward the fishing boats and warehouses.

It was another brisk night, made all the more so by the damp air near the waterfront. Brunelle put his hands in his pockets and turned down some unnamed alley toward the water. The sight of Salmon Bay at night might ease his nerves while he waited for Chen's call.

Although he was starting to think that call would never come. Or at least when it finally did come, it would be to report that their gambit had failed. So when his ringer went off as he approached Shilshole Avenue, he felt more trepidation than excitement.

He pulled the phone out of his pocket and pressed it to his ear. "Brunelle," he answered.

"Dave! What the hell are you doing?" It was Chen's voice, but not anything Brunelle had expected to hear.

"What?" he replied. "What do you mean?"

"You're walking right into the stake-out," Chen answered. "Montero just called me. They tracked Brown to Ballard, but you're about to blow the whole thing. Get the hell out of there!"

"Fuck." Brunelle looked around. He didn't see anyone, but

that was kind of the point, he supposed. It was a dark, desolate area. No retail or eating establishments. Just docks and warehouses and barely paved alleyways. Perfect for a mind-clearing walk. And maybe also for disposing of a body. "Uh, Okay. Shit. I'll get out of here. Sorry. I just—"

"Just shut up and get the hell out of there," Chen ordered. "Fuck. We may have to abort the whole thing if he saw you."

Brunelle shook his head. "I don't think anyone saw me."

"Montero did, you idiot," Chen growled. "Get the fuck out of there."

"Shit." Brunelle said. "Shit, shit. Okay. Fuck. Damn it."

He hung up and spun his head around. Go back the way he came? Well, that's where they spotted him, so that was probably a bad idea. He'd just walk through the stake-out again. Another frantic glance around the area. There was a warehouse parking lot he could cut through if it wasn't fenced on the other side. That would get him back to Ballard Way and he could head back north on a main road.

"Fuck," he whispered as he darted into the parking lot. It was bad enough he'd messed up the entire case. Now he was about to mess up his one chance to rescue it. He lowered his head and hurried into the dark of the unlit parking lot. He really hoped there was no fence on the other side of the building. If there was, he might just sit down against it and wait for everything to end. Like his career.

Brunelle looked up at the three-story-tall warehouse as he walked through the back lot. It was definitely closed. In fact, it was abandoned. Well, abandoned might be a strong word. It was Seattle after all, not Detroit. But it was vacant. Several commercial 'For Sale' signs were posted on the sides and windows. Brunelle wondered absently how difficult it might be to lease a warehouse on the waterfront in a fishing district. That had to be a small market of potential renters. A place like that might sit empty for months, even years. Suddenly, he was glad he was a prosecutor again and not a commercial fisheries real estate agent.

As he approached the far end of the parking lot, he was not at all surprised to see that it was in fact fenced off from its neighbors. It was a short enough fence though, with no razor wire on top, so he stopped for a moment to consider whether he should try to climb over it. He looked down. Chen was right: he did always wear a suit. He didn't relish climbing a chain link fence in a coat and tie. He scanned for other options. To his surprise, he found one.

There was a section where the fence had been pulled away from the fence-pole. It led into a darkened, lightly wooded area. Based on his location, Brunelle was pretty sure Ballard Way would be on the other side of it. His suit would probably fare better pushing through some thin trees than getting snagged on the top of a chain link fence.

He pulled the curled fence section back with a metallic rattle and stepped into the dark. He only hoped he'd gotten out of the way in time to let Montero finish the operation. He suddenly let himself get excited again. If they had followed Brown, that meant the ruse had worked. Maybe the cops would catch Brown red-handed, digging up the shallow grave he'd used to conceal Amy Corrigan's body.

Or, Brunelle realized as he pushed past another sapling and into a small clearing, maybe he would be the one to catch Brown red-handed.

Kenny Brown looked up from where he had just unearthed what was nauseatingly clear was Amy Corrigan's arm. Several months concealed under high-water-table soil had managed to liquefy most of the flesh into a muddy gelatin. Brunelle had just enough time to notice that Amy's metal bracelet hadn't decomposed and to consider that the gelatin would still have Amy's DNA in it. Then Kenny Brown dropped his shovel and pulled out his .45 semi-auto.

"You!" Brown yelled. "What the fuck are you doing here?"

Under different circumstances, Brunelle might have tried a witty rejoinder like, 'I was just about to ask you the same thing.' But confronted with the smell of Amy's rotten corpse and the sight of Brown's leveled handgun, Brunelle did the only thing that made sense. He turned and ran.

The shot was louder than he expected somehow. It was more like a stabbing in his ears than an actual noise. Pain rather than sound. But it was nothing compared to the pain that tore through his left thigh as the bullet ripped through his leg. He fell face first into the mud, unable to move and certain he was going to die.

He waited for a second shot, but it didn't come. Instead, he lay in the dark, feeling the blood pump from his leg with every heartbeat. Brown must have fled. He knew enough from reading medical and autopsy that he'd been hit in the artery. Some fucking artery in the thigh whose name he couldn't quite remember. But it was big and his heart was pumping blood through it directly into the mud beneath him.

He reached down, gritting his teeth against the fire in his leg and the dizziness in his head, and pulled the phone from his pocket. He tapped the screen and scrolled to the phone app. Chen was the last one to call him. He could just call him back. And that's when his phone battery gave out.

His phone died.

Brunelle closed his eyes, laid his face back into the mud, and prepared to do the same.

EPILOGUE

When Brunelle woke up, he was in a hospital bed. His mouth was dry. There was an I.V. stuck into the back of his hand. His leg hurt like hell.

And Chen was across the room, sitting in a chair, reading a paperback.

Brunelle swallowed, painfully, and tried to speak. "Larry?" he croaked.

Chen jumped to his feet, dropping the book on the floor. "Dave! Dave, are you okay?"

Brunelle squinted against the fluorescent lights and scanned his surroundings. "I guess not. What the hell happened?"

"You got shot," Chen answered. "Brown shot you in the leg. But we caught him. When they heard the shot, Montero and the others were on him like stink on shit."

Brunelle started to remember. "A—Amy?"

"We found the body," Chen confirmed. "Brown is done. Grissom declared a mistrial and he's getting arraigned this afternoon on attempted murder."

Brunelle was still groggy. "Only attempted?"

Chen laughed slightly. "For you, dummy. He's going down on murder one for Amy now for sure. You did it."

Brunelle closed his eyes and leaned back into his pillow. "Good," he half-whispered.

"You lost a lot of blood, buddy," Chen told him. "You're lucky we found you so quick."

Brunelle nodded slightly, but didn't open his eyes. "Thanks."

"Hold on," Chen said. "There's somebody else who'll want to see you're okay."

Brunelle nodded again, eyes still closed. A moment later he heard Kat's voice. "Hey, you."

Brunelle's eyes flew open. Kat and Chen were on either side of his bed.

"You're supposed to let the cops get shot at," she joked. "I don't want you ending up on my examining table."

Brunelle managed a smile. "You know Larry can't do anything right. He needs a little help from his friends."

Kat nodded, then reached out and took Brunelle's hand. "We all do."

Brunelle was exhausted. His leg hurt. He was still trying to remember everything that had happened. But he squeezed Kat's hand. "Friends?" he asked.

Kat nodded. "Of course," she answered. "We'll always be friends."

Brunelle leaned back and closed his eyes. That was good enough for him.

END